Fireside STORIES

A Heartwarming Collection of Short Stories from the West

by
John Patrick Gillese

LONE
PINE

©1997 by Lone Pine Publishing

First Printed in 1997   5   4   3   2   1

Printed in Canada

The Publisher:
LONE PINE PUBLISHING

#206, 10426-81 Avenue	202A, 1110 Seymour Street	16149 Redmond Way, #180
Edmonton, AB	Vancouver, BC	Redmond, WA
Canada T6E 1X5	Canada V6B 3N3	U.S.A. 98052

Typsetting by Pièce de Résistance Typographers, Edmonton, Alberta

Printed by Best Book Manufacturers, Toronto, Ontario

Canadian Cataloguing in Publication Data
Gillese, John Patrick, 1926-
    Fireside stories

    Originally published under title: John Patrick Gillese's western gold.
    ISBN 1-55105-100-1

    I. Title. II. Title: John Patrick Gillese's western gold. III.
Title: Western gold.
PS8563.I486J64 1997   C813'.54   C96-910708-0
PR9199.3.G5299J64 1997

The publisher gratefully acknowledges the support of Alberta Community Development and the Department of Canadian Heritage.

Contents

Author's Foreword

This collection of short stories is for the West's pioneers—what few are left of them. It is for their sons and daughters, many in number, who are haunted by memories of a life they barely remember—haunted even more so by the people of an era whose flavour, I feel, can only be invoked by the small number of writers who had any success in capturing it through the printed word.

The original temptation (common to authors) was to select the ''best'' stories (always a very personalized judgement) out of a lifetime of writing. However, a lot of the stories herein appeared in a representative number of U.S. and Canadian magazines, the titles of which may not even be familiar to a new generation of readers.

I include among them *Collier's*—once, with the *Saturday Evening Post*, the mecca of all writers; the *Star Weekly* of Toronto, in the days when it was a ''broadsheet'' and was delivered dutifully by carrier in every fair-sized city in Canada; the *Family Herald* that in its heyday boasted over a million readers; the *Country Guide*, published by the United Grain Growers from Winnipeg. . . .

What did my ''bushwhacker'' stories have that fascinated—and I use the word deliberately—such an incredibly varied audience? *Capper's Farmer* in the U.S. and *Famille Blad* in Denmark were among many remote publications equally fascinated; in fact, I was selling bush country stories to *Capper's* for $75 (this at the tail-end of the depression) when the best you could expect from a Canadian publication was $20 to perhaps $50 or so.

As the recently-retired director of Alberta Culture's Film and Literary Arts branch, I like to think that what my stories ''had'' was good literary skills. I also assume I was lucky enough to stumble upon a fresh background—the bush country. American critic Riley Hughes, when he included one story (not in this collection) in his *All Manner of Men*, observed: "The author clearly knows his material . . . the fragrances and vistas of the Alberta bushland. Further, he knows his craft. . . ."

But I don't think that alone explains the appeal of these stories— an appeal that still manifests itself, as works are dug out of obscurity in a manner I know not how, and are reprinted in general-interest magazines and, more frequently of late, in a large number of school texts (Holt, Rinehart & Winston, Ginn, Academic Press, etc.). It is this interest by the grandsons and granddaughters of the pioneers that leads me to believe people are experiencing fresh hunger for their incredibly colourful past.

One of the problems in selecting the stories was to decide on which ones! Life in the bush country was—in its reality—a strange mixture of hope and disappointment, of ready acceptance and utter rejection, of dreams that were beautiful and brave but which, for the most part, were to be realized only in the lives of the generation that followed.

Was there ever such a man as the "Horseshoe" Hannigan of "Bushwhacker's Christmas"? I *know* there was! Not that many Christmasses ago, a young lady phoned me from the University of Alberta, with a message from her mother and father. The gist of it went like this:

"They really enjoy your short stories and would like you to come up and visit them any time. You can come for supper, or stay for a weekend, or my dad will take you on a moose hunt if you want."

Then a pause: "But my mother wants to know: how did you know her life story?"

I tried to explain that it only *seemed* I knew her mother's story— that the background was so authentic, it made the events seem true. But the girl cut me off: "Mr. Gillese, my mother was the young teacher—and she did marry the Chairman of the Board of School Trustees. . . ."

There were other telephone calls, more difficult to explain than that. In one story I had the mother's maiden name right, the proper brothers and sisters (though with different names) and a dog in the story with the same name as *her* dog—"Bunts." I still wet my lips nervously as I tell you I have only used one dog ever in a short story—and I haven't the foggiest notion why I named that one "Bunts." (But I did *not* know her mother or her family—or her dog!)

Obviously there are going to be slight exaggerations of the people who laugh and love and mourn in these stories. But some of the real events in the bushland were far more unbelievable than any in this "fiction'—and there were characters so bizarre that nobody would believe them in print, either in fact or in fiction.

The characters in these stories were drawn from people I knew (though in the mystery of fiction writing, *rarely* in the particular dramas in which they star here). Yet some of them are almost untouched from the real-life situations that gave them birth—the old lady who smoked a pipe, for instance, long before the feminist movement made the uncaring a little more recognizant of the right of women to be themselves. More spectacular still is the story behind "The Washing Machine." (See the italicized commentary with the story, and you will see what I mean.)

I suspect it was these characters that gave the bushwhacker stories their appeal. Because in retrospect I see them now: people who came to Canada's last agrarian frontier in search of a dream, because they couldn't "make it" back east or over in "the old country," a few who had barely escaped the police in Russia or even the U.S. and became model citizens . . . people who, in many ways, were like children: ready to laugh, easily moved to tears—but with a greatness of soul we may never see again.

A lot of people have asked me over the years "when" I was going to get out a collection of "your bushwhacker stories." Well, collections of short stories are really only coming into vogue now. But when one woman wrote, while I was still with Alberta Culture, that she and her husband had sought high and low (on the assumption they had been published in book form) for them for her parents' golden wedding anniversary, my mind was made up. "They used to live for your stories," she wrote. "My father read every story of yours from the very first . . ." and incredibly she listed titles that I would never have believed anyone could remember.

That brought the basic problem into focus: *which ones?* I could have occupied half this book with what I call "the Wrycjoski series" alone. But I wanted more . . .

The sons and daughters of the pioneers left home—some never to return, some to seek their own fortunes in a rapidly changing West . . . they needed to be in, too. Trying to be actors and newspapermen and stockbrokers—some of them remembering their bushland home . . . a few returning.

In honesty, I wrote many of the first stories accidentally: a writer usually stumbles onto the field in which he will find greatest acceptance. But once aware of what was happening, I tried to do what a writer really has an obligation to do: capture the essence of a time and place. So the setting of the stories ranges from the days of sod shacks and oxen, through the nigh-impossible chances of a woman winning in provincial politics . . . from the first boy leaving the bushland for university . . . and all the way through birth, the problems that followed the baby boom . . . and finally the grandchildren who never think (or at least rarely) of the bushland where, even for them, it all began.

I hope you enjoy meeting all of them. And with humility rare to writers, I hope this book serves as some sort of memorial to the people among whom I was raised—a wonderful and warm-hearted people . . . people whose like I will never know again.

◆◆◆◆

Woman Alone

As a boy growing up in the Alberta bushland, I wrote letters for many people, not all of them single and alone. I neither disliked the "chore" nor felt flattered by it: it was just something you did because you were a neighbour. . . . The reason I got a job stooking wheat (300 acres for $30 cash in 1937) and thus earned enough to buy my first typewriter, was because the widow who owned the land wanted somebody to write her letters (on Sundays). And there really was a woman "alone" in Indianapolis, Indiana, U.S.A.

What should a man do when suddenly he gets a letter from a woman he once loved, a woman he thinks he has shut out of his life forever?

Jim Acker kept right on milking his favourite cow, the old Jersey he had bought from my father when he first took land on Sucker Creek. Not till we had separated the milk and set the cream out to cool did he gesture me into the sitting room.

"It was neighbourly of you to make a special trip down with my mail, Jodie. Now I'll trouble you to read that letter to me."

He spoke casually, but it was only on special occasions Jim ever went into the front room at all. The time he had wasted fixing it up with a stone fireplace, my father often said, he could have cleared another ten acres easy.

"The woman who wrote this," Jim went on, handing me the letter and motioning me to sit in the handmade willow rocker, "taught me to sign my name, add a few figures—enough to get by. Ain't nobody knows but you that I can't really read or write. So get to it, boy."

It didn't seem right for me to be opening that envelope. It smelled faintly of lavender and it was postmarked Indianapolis, Indiana—a long way from where the bushland breeze was stirring the black balms on Sucker Creek. But it wasn't mannerly to argue with a neighbour, either. I tore open the end.

The first thing that fell out was a snapshot of a beautiful woman seated on a high-backed chair, with two young boys standing beside her.

Jim Acker looked at it almost impersonally. Then he rummaged in a drawer and came back with another photo. It was the same woman all right—only younger. She wore a wedding dress—the old-fashioned kind—of white satin with sweetheart bows.

"Emily Anderson," Jim said, as if he was introducing us. "Emily Loring now. Let's hear what she wants, Jodie. Somebody has to read this for me. I'd depend on you as ready as most."

I can still see that generous and sensitive script. Right now I can feel something of what Emily Loring felt when she sat down and wrote to a man she had not seen for 15 years.

She began by saying she did not know if Jim was still on his homestead in the Alberta bush country, or if he had found a woman worthy to be his wife.

"She knows," Jim said. "She knows I've never married—or she'd 'a died before writing me. What's she after, Jodie?"

I read: "It is three years past since Kimball passed away, leaving me with Billy, now eleven, and Alan, seven. I will never be able to educate them—I cannot even support them properly now. Daddy lost everything in the bank failure and is terribly embittered. Moreover, Alan is like his father, subject to lung trouble. . . ."

In brief, Emily Loring wondered if it would be possible for her and the boys to come to the Alberta bush country. Any work that would provide "a home for them and clothes for my own back" would be acceptable to her. The Alberta air, she thought, would do wonders for Alan's health.

"How do you reckon a woman?" Jim said. "As if all those years had never been!"

There was a smile on his lips—half-bitter, half-mocking. He moved back to the kitchen, troubled, and put a couple of pieces of sun-dried split poplar in the stove. While the coffee was brewing, we carried the pails of skim milk to his pigs.

I spilled it for the squealing feeders, kneeing them aside so I could pour. Jim fed his old sow. Usually he had a word for her. But now when she raised her rough head to be scratched, he growled at her.

"Go on, you old brute, and let me think."

He sat for a minute on the pigpen poles, squinting up at his cabin, as if trying to visualize what it would be like with someone else lighting the coal-oil lamp in the window and a couple of growing boys to slop the pigs and go fishing in the creek. Or maybe he was remembering when he first built it, choosing that spot in the old spruce. My mother always said he picked the prettiest site for a cabin there ever was. He was a man any woman could have been proud to marry, my mother always said.

"I built it for her," Jim said, picking up the slop pails again. "You're not 20 yet, Jodie, but some day I reckon you'll understand that that's what hurts now."

I understood some things. Why Jim's mail was only a farm weekly or the Eaton's catalogue. The paper he got for appearances, I guess. He'd always "troubled" my mother to order for him from the catalogue. I understood why he hardly ever visited or went to dances. The few times he did he'd stand on the sidelines, scarcely even hearing the neighbours' talk. Then, when all the women were swirling gaily to a square, he'd slip away. Sometimes even when he was right in our yard and Mom called supper, he'd excuse himself for not stopping to eat.

You could tell, all right, that Jim had a "past" too—like the postmaster, who'd been a hanging sheriff in the States—like even my own dad who'd left behind a pile of debts and discouragement. Up there we never talked openly about people's past troubles, though, unless the people themselves did the talking.

Back in the cabin, it seemed Jim Acker had to talk at last.

"This Kimball Loring was a band-leader—grew up with her. But it was her father that did it. He never did think I was right for her—especially when I decided to come up here, where land was free and a man's life was whatever he worked to make it."

I did what all the homesteaders did when people started to talk like that. I listened.

"Emily," Jim said, "she didn't rightly know her own mind from one week to the next. First she was all for running off and getting married. Then she thought maybe if I came up here and built a home . . ."

He smiled wanly.

"She was the most impulsive girl you ever saw—like a kid sometimes. That's how come we bought that wedding dress—she was going to bring it up here, so we'd have a real wedding, she said. It was her idea to get photographed in it, too—so I'd have something to work for every time I looked at it," Jim Acker said.

He shrugged a little. "Seems kind of crazy now, don't it? You can't file a homestead and build a cabin in one year . . ." He shrugged again. "And no amount of talking ever makes it the same."

We had coffee and bannock. Then Jim pushed back the cups and fetched writing paper from the front room. "I'll be obliged to you, Jodie, if you'll scrape off an answer."

I remember the stilted way he began, thanking Emily for her "kind letter and sorry to hear of your loss and circumstances."

With difficulty he went on: "My life is half over now. I am not married, nor can I say I have welcomed the thought of that state of late years. I do not wish to be unkind. But you've changed and I've changed and it is better to face that fact."

"Dictating," for Jim Acker, was harder than grubbing out poplar.

"Jus' tell her straight," Jim said, "There's no place at all in homesteading country for a woman alone. It wouldn't look right if she came up here as my housekeeper. The only way I see for her to bring the boys up here is to come up prepared to marry me."

The words out, he relaxed a little.

"Tell her the truth—that I'm not fussy about that side of it any more. She can sleep upstairs and I can sleep down. But it's not charity or pity that prompts me to offer her a home. I got nobody to leave the place to—nobody that cares—and I get tired of my own baching and talking to the old sow."

He advised Emily to "think it over without any persuasion of the past." If she wanted to come on those terms, she would be assured of a home. Her boys would not be treated unkindly—and one day they would have his land. It was more a proposal of trade than of marriage, but it was the best Jim Acker could do.

I often wonder what Emily Loring thought when she got that letter. Maybe she felt something of the same bittersweet heartache Jim Acker knew—like a kid who's missed a party, then finds somebody has saved a bit of cake for him, anyway. For Jim, nothing could ever be the same again. I am absolutely certain he didn't really care whether Emily Loring decided to come now or stay.

My folks didn't inquire too deeply into what writing I had done for Jim. He told them the barest details. They listened without comment. Up there, silence was the first law of respect. But it didn't mean they didn't care when a neighbour was troubled. Even though it was haying time, they sent me to the post office at least twice a week.

On an afternoon when the young prairie chickens were trying their first flights across the dirt roads, I got a lavender-scented letter from Indianapolis again. I took it across the line fence to where Jim was raking slough hay.

As if it was the last thing in the world that concerned him, he finished out the windrow before hearing the letter.

My Dear, Dear Jim (Emily Loring began). *I do not know whether I am a woman without shame—or a woman who has at last grown up. I was 19 when you went away, Jim. I am well past 30 now. So my life is almost half-over, too. And while I do not complain, it has not been an easy half.*

In the way we must communicate now, I cannot express my thoughts that made me dare to hope when I wrote to you again.

You know that Kimball was never strong. After our marriage he was often away. For the last three years he was almost constantly ill. He was a good man, Jim, and his greatest worry was about his sons. But how shall I make you believe that my heart was often caught with other dreams that might have come true had I not been such a foolish girl?

If I am to come as your wife, Jim, do I dare beforehand to ask you one question? Is there always to be the shadow of the foolish girl between us? Could I make you believe that God does not always grant happiness in years? Is it not true that sometimes, when we are older and wiser and perhaps better able to appreciate it, He offers it to us again—in generous, overflowing measure . . .

"You needn't read no more, Jodie," Jim Acker said. "She's coming."

I handed him the letter and he got up from the sticky warmth of the wild meadow. He climbed up on the hotter metal of the rake.

"She's coming. But I wonder. I guess," he said, "I'll always wonder."

It was Sunday before he asked me to stop by, if it was convenient. He dictated one more letter to Emily Loring—tighter, more terse, than the first.

She could suit herself when she came, but he opined it would be better if it was before Indian summer ended. That way, the Alberta winter wouldn't seem so long.

She would find the cabin a mess. He didn't have time to fix it up. As soon as haying was over, he'd have to get to cutting and threshing. But under the circumstances it would give her and the boys something to occupy themselves with till freeze-up.

The neighbours would accept her for what she was. He would be on hand to meet the train if she would let him know, in good time, the exact day she would arrive.

The threshing had started and prairie chickens were calling *tuk-alok* on the wheat stooks the afternoon we drove to the railway. Jim had asked me to go with him to town. I think he was plain scared to meet Emily alone.

"She would pick a time like this—I'm needed for the spike-pitching at Walters'.'' It was a wonderful harvest day. September had smeared colour all over the bushland, from Sucker Creek to the railway tracks and over the poplar-inflamed hills beyond. ''Might be best, Jodic, if after we get it over with, you drive her down to the flats and I cut over the fields to Walters'.''

I didn't say anything. Jim Acker wasn't talking to me anyway.

On Fraemar's hill, from where you could see the grain elevator roofs above the burnished bush, he spoke to me more directly.

''You read a lot Jodie. How do you think these kind of things turn out?''

''They turn out the way people want them to, I guess.''

Jim looked at me sideways. Wearing his Sunday clothes, he looked uncomfortable in the September sun. ''It's different when you're starting fresh without all those years in between—''

''Jim,'' I said, seeing again the letters I was never supposed to see, ''ain't you forgetting one thing?''

''What's that?'' Jim said, surprised.

''How scared she is, too.''

Jim stood up in the buggy and yelled ''Giddup!'' at his horses.

The train was late. We wandered up and down the streets to the station. The town was always empty at threshing time. This time it was a frightening emptiness—like, I thought, the emptiness in Jim Acker's heart.

We had wandered down to the station for the fifth time; and as if it was a cue, the train whistle sounded on the trestle to the east. Jim Acker stopped as if he had been frozen to the cinders.

The postmaster appeared on the platform, ready to receive the incoming mail. He nodded, without speaking, and absently fingered the revolver on his hip. He was the only man, other than the Alberta Provincial Police constable, allowed to wear a gun. He was responsible not only for the post office money, but for the grain elevator money as well. Each fall, the farmers cashed their grain cheques in the post office.

The postmaster picked the spot where the baggage car would stop. The station agent pushed open the green door of the depot and joined him. They did not want to embarrass Jim by looking our way.

Jim Acker rubbed his sweating palms on his good jacket.

With a vibration that made the piled-up cream cans rattle, the old bush-country freight thundered by: a half-mile of white-barred cattle cars, dark-red grain cars, a soot-green baggage car and a single, cinder-dusty passenger coach before the wobbling red caboose.

"Fifteen years!" Jim Acker whispered, as if he was only realizing now what he had done.

Two boys, in knee-length pants and gray caps, were stepping down to the platform. The oldest one—Billy Loring—turned to help his mother down.

I felt as if, inside, I was going to explode. Beside me, Jim Acker gasped.

It wasn't the sight of Emily Loring—her face bright, her head high. It wasn't the way she looked toward the depot, then turned to where we stood, almost at the platform's end.

It was the dress she wore—the most beautiful dress I had ever seen in my life—a white satin wedding dress with sweetheart bows.

Somehow I went over to the boys. But Jim Acker couldn't make it. Emily Loring had to go to him.

There was no marriage that day. Nor did I drive Emily to Jim Acker's cabin on Sucker Creek. At Jim's request, I took her home to be my mother's guest for the threshing.

That night, after spike-pitching was done for another day, after the cows were milked and the pigs fed, Jim Acker got out a scrub pail and started in on the cabin floor. I found him there on his knees when I took down the first pie Emily Loring ever baked in the bush country.

"Like you said, Jodie"—he tried to explain the scrubbing—"it never will be anything if you don't at least start out right."

"She says to come up and see her, Jim," I said. "She says the house can wait."

His face was dazed. "She still got that dress on?"

I told him she had borrowed one of my mother's. She had put the other one away, till she was sure, as she put it, of the wedding.

"Damn-fool thing to wear up here, among all these neighbours of mine." Jim Acker said. But when he got to his feet, he was kind of grinning.

"You'd think, Jodie," he said, "that even a woman like Emily would get some sense after all these years."

Whatever you wanted to think, Jim Acker came, hat in hand, to our place to court her. And it was a different wedding than he'd planned, too. It was in my mother's parlour, with my dad *attending* Jim and my mother wearing *her* old wedding dress.

I had to cut out hearts to decorate our living room. Then I had to drive Jim Acker and his bride—and family—home.

My mother daubed at her eyes when I told her Jim had carried Emily in his arms across the threshold.

You'd have thought, my father said, that a fellow who'd carried logs off the clearing for 15 years would have got over such nonsense long ago.

Bushwhacker's Christmas

Every new teacher graduating from Normal School in Edmonton was sent to the bush country. This is the story that prompted one of them to inquire, via her daughter graduating from the University of Alberta, how I knew her story.

When I was a kid growing up around Dogberry Creek, education was a problem. In the first three years after the log schoolhouse was built, we had exactly ten teachers—all women. Neither isolation nor the hardships of life in the Alberta bush country caused them to quit their jobs. They all got married.

As always in time of crisis, the valley called on Horseshoe Hannigan—a giant of a man and, as I remember him, a legendary figure in our valley settlement. Horseshoe's first official act, as Chairman of the Board of School Trustees, was to ask the latest applicant for teacher—a Miss Elda Keene, from Edmonton—if she would promise to teach out a full term of school and not worry any of the parents of the valley by looking, at any time, as if she might get married.

Elda Keene's reaction was highly encouraging.

"I wouldn't marry one of these bushwhackers," she said scornfully, "for a—for a million dollars."

"That's the spirit," approved Horseshoe, and hired her—salary $500 a year (cash) plus board and lodging with Sam Bigelow's widow. The widow's cabin was only a mile from school, and Horseshoe assured Miss Keene that if the drifts got bad in winter, the School Board would provide a horse.

This done, Hannigan went back to the upper reaches of Dogberry, leaving it to Ray and MacGregor, the other members of the Board of School Trustees, to deal with such lesser problems as correspondence with Edmonton, janitor work, and the buying of chalk and erasers. They were, said Hannigan, only to bother him if anything serious arose.

Towards the end of October, Ray and MacGregor summoned Hannigan to a special Saturday night board meeting. They had ominous signs to report. Miss Keene had gone out three Saturdays running with young Jesse Kramer, who kept the combination store and post office.

It was a night with a strong taste of black frost and old leaves in the air. One of those crisp late fall nights in Alberta when a man's mind turns to thoughts of beavers trailing boughs under the cold moon . . . of sap-scented hollows where the leaves are molding . . . of tired hills and thickening river water . . . and the smell of fur on your back as nightfall brings you home.

Horseshoe was forced to think, instead, of how hard it would be to get a fill-in teacher in the middle of winter, and in the bright of the following Sunday, he walked the six miles downriver from his cabin to the Widow Bigelow's.

Elda Keen was curled up on the old horsehair sofa reading a book. She was tall, with a trick of laughing at you with her eyes. This Sunday she wore a green ribbon that made you notice her soft dark hair.

Horseshoe paid his respects to the Widow Bigelow, while he surveyed Elda Keene surreptitiously in an effort to determine what made teachers so unreliable. Two things the other ten teachers all had in common, he remembered—their looks and their age.

"You got it, too," said Hannigan, aloud, and not very happily.

Miss Keene lowered her book, uncrossed her legs and sat up with interest.

"What have I got, Mr. Hannigan?" she asked sweetly.

"I was just thinkin'," said Hannigan. "Miss Keene, I've got to talk to you. In private," he added, to the suddenly interested widow. "This here's school business."

The widow withdrew, reluctantly.

Hannigan, usually the most affable of men, tried to look severe.

"Miss Keene, this ain't personal. It's about your work."

"How is my work?" asked Elda Keene quickly. "Satisfactory, I hope?"

"As far as teachin' goes, it's fine," said Hannigan, sweating a little. "Everyone I talk to says their kids is gettin' along fine—"

"Are getting along well," corrected Elda Keene.

Horseshoe looked blank.

"Mr. Hannigan," said Elda Keene, "it seems to me you use

atrocious English for a man who is Chairman of the Board of School Trustees.''

"Well," said Hannigan, in surprise, "that's only natural. I ain't never had no education."

"And in what way, then," asked Elda sweetly, "are you qualified for your job? I suppose you can neither read nor write—"

"Do I gotta be a hen to know a good egg?" asked Hannigan defensively. "Anyways, I got a sense of responsibility to my job—"

The schoolteacher coloured. She got to her feet and shook her dark hair once—just like a mink getting ready to do battle, Horseshoe thought.

"Just exactly what do you mean by that, Mr. Hannigan?''

"I mean," said Hannigan, determined to see it through, "your goin' out with that young whippersnapper, Jesse Kramer. That guy talks to every woman he sees an' never means a word of it. Maybe he is the best-dressed guy in the valley—he oughta be, seein' he runs the store—but you gave me your word—"

"I am also going to give you a piece of my mind," said Elda Keene furiously. "In the first place, what am I supposed to do to amuse myself? Grub stumps or trap a moose?''

"You don't trap moose—" interjected Horseshoe, but Elda wasn't to be stopped.

"All right, I told you I wouldn't marry a bushwhacker. Well, Jesse is no bushwhacker! He's a—a gentleman—"

"There you go!" Horseshoe yelled bitterly. "Trap me on a technicality. You're just talkin' the talk of wimmen in love. First they hate everybody—wouldn't marry 'em for a million dollars. Then they're hoppin' mad at anybody what even tries to give 'em a piece of advice. Then they just lose their senses an' marry an' upset everything."

This went on, by the widow's calculations, for exactly one hour. First the teacher yelled at Hannigan. Then Hannigan yelled at the teacher. It was real exciting, the widow said. The only part she neglected to tell the community was Hannigan's injunction that the talk was official business.

Horseshoe waited, with a sense of fatal premonition, to see the effects of his talk. He was cutting for bear signs the day he returned to the cabin to find Ray and MacGregor waiting.

"Tell me the worst," said Hannigan haggardly.

They told him. Jesse had taken Elda out—in the middle of the week. Even the other teachers had never betrayed their trust to the extent of "going out" other than during the approved recreation time for teachers—Saturday nights.

"Leave me be," said Horseshoe, with the stoic fortitude of a man who knows his duty. "I'll think of something."

It snowed that night. Listening to the muted music of it tattering down the valley, a daring idea came to Hannigan. For a moment, it took his breath away. Then, resolutely, he squared his chin and decided to talk it over with Ray and MacGregor.

They listened. And when he had done, they looked at him with the reverence given only to men of genius.

The next Sunday, Horseshoe again hiked downriver, icing now and black, to the Widow Bigelow's. A red fox skin, which he had tanned himself, was under his arm. Elda, wearing her winter-like clothes, received him with wary politeness.

Hannigan gave her a reassuring grin.

"I been thinkin', Miss Keene. 'Twasn't very polite of me to be comin' over here an' gettin' mad at you—"

The schoolteacher looked a little less suspicious.

"So I brought you this," concluded Hannigan, with slight embarrassment, "just to show you I'm sorry for the way I acted."

Elda took the fox skin wonderingly. She caressed it.

"It's beautiful!" she whispered, almost to herself. Her eyes lifted. "Thank you, Mr. Hannigan! I'm sorry, too—so let's forget it. Tell me how you ever caught this beautiful fox."

Fur was a subject dear to Hannigan's heart. Without fear now, he could let himself go. He explained to Elda that, in his opinion, red fox was the prettiest of all the fox furs. A silver fox, said Hannigan, was nothing but a freak on the part of Mother Nature—an off-colour red. And not half as smart, either. He explained how baby foxes played like puppies, how they chewed on old bones to cut their teeth, what they ate, how they could dart down groundhog holes, and how they bit each other's tails and raced around stumps when the winter moon was white.

"My goodness," said Elda, her eyes big. "You know a lot about foxes, Mr. Hannigan!"

The afternoon proceeded smoothly, much to the amazement of the Widow Bigelow, who had never known Horseshoe to speak more than a single sentence to any woman. As dusk fell, Hannigan left for his lonely cabin up the Dogberry. On the dark edge of the shrouded forest, he turned to look back. Elda was standing in the doorway, framed in the light of the coal-oil lamp. She waved to him—and smiled slowly.

Hannigan was aware of a queer feeling in the pit of his stomach. He put it down to the widow's biscuits. "She never was a cook," he reflected; and wondered, sagely, if perchance the other teachers had got married merely to escape living with her. He would, he decided, bring it up at the next regular board meeting.

Friday, after school, Elda went skiing with Jesse Kramer. The way they told it to the Chairman of the Board of School Trustees, it was apparent that Elda had never skied before in her life and Jesse had to be always helping her up and keeping his arm around her waist to give her confidence.

Horseshoe mentioned the matter—casually—to Elda, as he was leaving the widow's on still another Sunday. It was colder; and Elda had donned an overcoat and a coloured tuque and was walking with him to the edge of bushland. Now she looked up at him and laughed.

"Oh, that! I just started thinking about what you said about the winter drifts and my needing a horse. I thought a pair of skis would be so much—neater. Wasn't it generous of Jesse to close up his store just to teach me?"

"Yeah!" growled Horseshoe, whose opinion of Jesse's athletic abilities was limited.

Elda took hold of his hand. It seemed to Horseshoe that an electric current shot through him.

"Horseshoe?" Elda murmured.

Hannigan managed to meet her eyes.

"Have you ever been in love?"

Hannigan managed to shake his head.

Elda smiled slowly. "Someday maybe you will be."

Horseshoe broke through some rapid-ice on the way home. It was the first time in his 20 years on the Dogberry that he had failed to notice dangerous river ice. In a way, he was beginning to understand what caused the other ten homesteaders to forget their obligations to the community and marry all available schoolteachers.

Fur signs were plentiful that winter, but, strangely enough, Horseshoe spent less time than usual tending his traps. He made repeated visits to the Widow Bigelow's, sometimes even in the middle of the week. He brought the widow a roast of venison; and a month before the Christmas concert, he gave Elda a pair of handmade skis. Elda accepted the gift graciously.

The first Sunday in December, when rainbow-hued sundogs made parentheses in the cold sky, he brought her a wild swan feather. She had been talking, the week before, of what she would wear for the concert. And on a far lake, he found the feather, caught in the frozen reeds.

"Thought it would look pretty in your hat," Horseshoe said.

To his surprise, she turned away. After a minute, she said, low enough so the widow couldn't overhear.

"Jesse has asked me to marry him."

Hannigan stood there. "You—you gonna?" he asked finally.

The dark head shook. "How can I? I—I don't love him."

The way Elda said "him," did something to Hannigan's heart. Suddenly he forgot about anxious parents, the appalling record of vacancies, the dire warnings from the Department of Education that if Dogberry Valley wanted their school grants continued, they would have to elect a more efficient School Board.

"Elda," Horseshoe said miserably, "don't listen to that guy. Elda—it's me that loves you. Marry me!"

Even the widow's presence couldn't stifle the cry of joy that fell from Elda's lips. She was, suddenly, no longer just a woman, but a woman apart—his. She threw her young arms around Horseshoe's neck and kissed him.

"Oh, Horseshoe!" she cried. "I love you, my darling! I do love you—so awfully much—how much you'll never know!"

Hannigan, though becoming used to little gestures of love, was still embarrassed by words of love. But that afternoon he did manage to suggest that he could have a new cabin up about the end of the teaching term—mid-June. He left in a daze, thinking only of the Christmas concert when he would see Elda again.

Elda stood in the doorway, oblivious to the freezing air, throwing kisses at Hannigan as his bulk disappeared towards the forest. The widow's voice brought her, finally, back to earth.

"There's talk goin' round, Eldy."

"Talk?" Elda turned vacantly, closed the door in a trance. "People needn't worry—I'll finish teaching the term." She closed her eyes and smiled. "Horseshoe's going to build on a spruce bluff overlooking the creek. He says the colours in autumn there—"

"They say," opined the widow, "that Horseshoe personally assured the School Board that he'd keep you from marrying Jesse Kramer if he had to make love to you himself."

"He—he did?" said Elda faintly.

"'Tain't my business," said the widow, "but I like you the best of 'em all, Eldy. Horseshoe never talked to a girl in his life till after he got so mad at you for going out with Jesse. . . ."

There was no pay for those who served as Chairman of the Board of School Trustees back there in that Alberta valley where I was raised. But there were compensating honours. One of them was the distinction of being Master of Ceremonies for the School Concert, of reading, from a sheet of foolscap, the titles of the recitations, songs and plays "next on the program," and calling out the names of those taking part—as if everyone hadn't known for weeks beforehand just who would do what on that long-looked-for night.

On arriving at the school, shining and scrubbed, Hannigan found, to his surprise, that Jesse Kramer had been asked to ''do the honours.'' The teacher was busy running in and out of the cloakroom pinning gauze wings on a fairy and cardboard stars on the angels.

However, as she rushed on some errand to the great shimmering Christmas tree at the back of the room, Horseshoe did manage to whisper a shy greeting of endearment.

Elda's smile, he thought, was somehow different than it had been the Sunday before. Loud enough, so that everybody two rows back could hear, Elda explained why she had asked Jesse Kramer to announce.

''Since you can't read or write, I thought I'd spare you the embarrassment.''

''I ain't that illiterate!'' Horseshoe whispered back, hurt more than he cared to admit.

Then, figuring she had enough worries with the kids, he managed a cover-up smile. ''Yeah, sure!'' he said. ''Jesse can do it a lot nicer, anyway—he can add all sorts of fancy extras that a guy like me would never think of.''

He sat there, as the coal-oil lamps, one by one, were blown out, until only the makeshift stage was lighted. Every person for miles around was there to see the kids act their pieces and to take part in the social evening to follow.

Watching the little ones up on the stage, hearing them sing the Christmas carols, seeing the mothers wiping their eyes and the fathers hardly able to tear their gaze away from the front, Horseshoe suddenly realized what Elda had brought into that valley.

''Si-i-lent night, Ho-o-ly night—'' trebled the little voices, and suddenly it was too much for Horseshoe. The loneliness of all his lonely years coursed through him in hurting waves. He was a part of the wilderness, as big as its hills, as deep as its rivers. His whole being was tuned to the moods of the seasons; and when Elda, in a brocaded white dress, slipped over to the piano to render a solo, it was springtime in Hannigan's heart. With the rest of them, he fought back the tears thickening his throat.

The lamps would not be relighted till after the Christmas tree was attended to. Quick tears had given way to quick laughter again. The concert was over, and Jesse Kramer announced to the anxious kids that Santa Claus was on his way and would arrive at any minute direct from the North Pole. This, Horseshoe knew, was to allow the chosen one time to get dressed, while not missing any of the concert. Inwardly, he had hoped that in recompense for his not being Master of Ceremonies, Elda would have asked him to act the part of Santa Claus.

When MacGregor came in instead, jangling bells, roaring Ho-Ho-Ho's that caused the kids' eyes to pop, Horseshoe rebuked himself mentally for always wanting to hog all the glory.

There was a gift for each school kiddy, as well as for the little ones still at home. And for each, a green net bag of candy and an orange. Santa did his job well, too, calling each child by name—in a voice that had a remarkable Scottish burr . . . pausing, as the mysterious parcels were brought from the highest branches of the tree, to tell funny tales that made even the grown-ups laugh.

Some people, Hannigan thought, with pride in his fellow board member, sure had the gift of talk.

It was then, as Santa began his farewell, and the lamps yellowed up again along the sides of the warm log schoolhouse, that Jesse Kramer returned to the stage, smiling and holding out his hands for attention.

"Folks, before you clear the benches out for dancing, I have a special announcement to make."

With the rest of them, Horseshoe looked up expectantly.

"I think you will agree with me," Jesse said dramatically, "that much of what we have to rejoice over in this valley, we owe to an outstanding and public-spirited citizen—who has never, ladies and gentlemen, hesitated to step forward in times of emergency and lend a hand. I am sure he will be equally happy now to come up here and, in his usual illustrious manner, say a few appropriate words to us tonight. Mr. Horseshoe Hannigan!"

For a moment, sheer and absolute terror, mingled with unbelief, froze Horseshoe to his seat. He looked around as if seeking a way of escape and saw only the faces of the good people of the valley smiling at him and clapping their applause.

"Horseshoe!" Jesse's face was wreathed in guileless smiles. "Come on up and say a few words."

It came to Hannigan then. This was Elda's idea. She had saved this for him and had forgotten to tell him. Or maybe she had just thought of it now, to make up for his not being Master of Ceremonies or Santa Claus.

Never in his life before had Hannigan made a speech. He had, as he himself described it, been a man who was never afraid to turn his hand to anything. He had dynamited logjams, rounded up wild horses, snowshoed 30 miles in a blizzard to get the nearest doctor for a sick neighbour. Yet never had he possessed the courage to stand up and talk before a crowd of people who knew him.

"Horseshoe!" They were yelling his name now, and clapping. One or two of his old cronies, sensing the fun it could be, were stomping their feet, whistling and yelling, "Speech! Speech!"

Hannigan got to his feet, moved by something stronger than himself.

Slowly and awkwardly, wishing he could think of witty jokes as fast as Jesse Kramer, he gazed down on the upturned faces of the crowd.

"Truth to tell, folks—ah—" It didn't even sound like his own voice. "I never figgered to make a speech. But I'm going to—though what I have to say won't take long—which is a good thing, too, I guess."

Thankfully, there was a brief snicker, which helped.

"First, the reason I'm gonna say it is this. All of you, nearly, have done something to make this worthwhile. A lot of you have kids up on the stage—I guess no one can equal that contribution."

Horseshoe swallowed. This was no good—this wouldn't make nobody laugh. "And—and'—Horseshoe desperately wracked his mind—'you men put up the tree and you women brought eats for the dance—and nobody would eat anything I cooked!"

The men laughed loudly. Encouraged by this response, Horseshoe could afford to feel that no matter what he said now, the speech couldn't be regarded as a complete failure.

"All I can do—folks—is say thanks for somethin' else. When I was sittin' there tonight, I knew what it was. How it happened, I'll never know. But three years ago, before we had this school, there was a barrenness in our lives. Now there's something else. We gave the kids candy and fruit—and a few little toys. Maybe we can never even think why we want to do that at Christmas time. Well, it's because they give us something else—like they gave us tonight—something spiritual, I guess you'd call it. Maybe it's like what they had in the play—the mysterious gifts of the Wise Men of the East—things you can't value like you would a red fox pelt—"

Horseshoe stopped, his tongue dry. While he was speaking, searching for words, he'd had his eyes fixed on the rafters. Now suddenly he saw that the schoolhouse was still. Except for the restless kids, nobody was moving. Nobody was even smiling any more. They were staring at him as if suddenly he had been transformed before their eyes.

Horseshoe, overwhelmed by the depth of his own thoughts, still couldn't be sure whether this was the attention reserved only for famous orators—or whether his neighbours thought he had lost his mind. Maybe some of them even figured he'd been working on the side and had acquired an education. Whatever it was, Horseshoe decided to appear completely at home on the speaker's platform. Deliberately he unbuttoned his shirt collar, shook his head sideways to widen the breathing space around his neck, took a deep breath of the spruce-fragrant air and concluded.

"There—there's something else I figger I ought to mention here. I'd just like to say, as Chairman of the Board of School Trustees, that at least part of what we felt tonight, we must owe, surely, to our schoolteacher. I reckon the goodness in teachers comes out in the kids—and so I know, you'll all give Miss Keene a hearty vote of thanks.''

It was done and he was outside—long before the yells of the crowd had subsided—gulping the freezing air into his lungs. Glad he'd done it, but glad with all his being that it was over.

Just one thing worried him—Elda. He had caught a glimpse of her face behind the curtains that served as stage wings. It was so white and stricken that he knew then something *was* wrong. Elda hadn't been proud of him—or even encouraging him with a smile. She had been standing beside Jesse Kramer as if in a daze.

Inside, the volunteer orchestra tuned up. The dancing commenced. There was the scrape of feet on the floor, the shouts, the laughter. It was cold under the freezing, glittering sky. Horseshoe went inside.

Elda was dancing with old Chris Johnson. Horseshoe talked to the homesteaders who didn't have girls, and laughed at their jokes, and pretended not to see when, as the second dance started, Elda quickly accepted MacGregor's arm.

At the Christmas tree concert, Horseshoe remembered, nobody went home till after lunch. He kept on laughing and appearing indifferent as Jesse called squares and reels and Elda always managed to get whisked up by the man nearest her. It was plain to see she was giving Horseshoe no chance to ask her to dance.

There came, inevitably, the expectant pause before the supper waltz. Jesse Kramer, smiling gaily, made the announcement from the floor.

"Because there are more gents than ladies here, folks—as usual!—we'll make this one Ladies' Choice—''

Jesse began to elbow his way towards Elda, who suddenly looked down the full length of the schoolroom floor. She walked towards Horseshoe Hannigan. There was a smile on her lips and her black hair was thrown back, tied with a gay green ribbon. He thought his heart would burst.

It was sweet music. It was the first time Horseshoe's arms had ever held her—indeed, the first time he had ever really held any woman. He tried to think of something to say, and no words would come.

"They tell me, Mr. Hannigan,'' said Elda, as if she had never kissed him once, "that you built this school.''

"Yeah," Horseshoe admitted, looking straight ahead. "Most of them's farmers—and the bushland's sure hard to clear. Me—well, trappers don't work hard in summer."

"Christian Johnson told me'—Elda's voice was brittle—'that you rescued him and his wife the spring they got trapped in the flood. You rode a horse in there and tied them both on it, and you hung onto the horse's tail till you got out."

"That was a powerful sudden flood," mumbled Horseshoe. "Doggoned Dogberry was rising four feet an hour."

"You're quite a hero, Mr. Hannigan," Elda said.

Horseshoe couldn't see into her eyes. But he could feel her body shaking. He said the words that, in his heart, he figured he would have had to say some day, anyway.

"Elda, Christmas is for givin'—so I'm giving you back to what you were before I came along. You're not obliged to remember last Sunday—not in this valley, where men are free. You were right, Elda— no bushwhacker's good enough for a woman who can make magic in people's lonely hearts. I would like to tell you, though—I didn't really mean to fall in love with you. I was scared to even think of it. But pretending I was doing it for the sake of the school—that kind of gave me the confidence to start."

"You told Mr. Ray and Mr. MacGregor!" Elda said furiously.

"Yeah," Horseshoe admitted. "I did. Don't you understand—I didn't want them laughing at me, when you'd gone away."

"I thought you were trying to make a fool of me," Elda whispered. "I wanted to do the same to you. I—I was going to teach on till June, and then go away and leave this valley forever, and never come back."

After awhile, it made sense to Horseshoe. "Why didn't you, then?"

"I fell in love with you—when you brought me that fox fur," Elda told him. "Then when you made that speech tonight, I knew I couldn't hurt you as I planned. I'm not worthy of you, Horseshoe—I'm the ignorant one here—not you or any of these others—"

"That's some talk," said Horseshoe, "for a woman who said she wouldn't marry a bushwhacker for a million dollars." He made her smile, and suddenly he knew it was Christmas time. He felt that all at once the gifts of old were flowing to him, as no one could ever know them, except a man at peace with himself and his fellow men.

Elda seemed to creep closer in his arms. She looked up and she was smiling. "Remember—I told you some day you'd fall in love, Tobias darling!"

"Tobias!" Hannigan gasped. "Elda, who told you that was my real name?"

Elda smiled dreamily. "Well, I knew nobody's mother ever

christened a child 'Horseshoe.' So I asked the widow, darling. . . .''

For years they used to tell around Dogberry Creek that when Horseshoe and Elda were married the following June, it was the largest and most beautiful wedding in the valley. There was even a rumour that after the wedding, the great Hannigan, faithful to his problems of office, made his bride promise that any time a schoolteacher decided to get married, she must be willing to fill in till a new one was found.

The Price of a Piano

There were at least two women that I knew of in the bush country who had achieved some fame in music (and both, in later years, taught piano to the children growing up around them). I remembered that someone had toted a piano up the mountains to the Klondike gold fields. I actually have phonograph records that are now antiques, brought into the bushland by the pioneers. Of all the "luxuries" that the first settlers had to leave behind, music was the hardest to forget. They sang the old-time songs clearing land, riding the wagon trails. A barn dance would bring them together, especially in the winter. Far from turning on TV sets, they did not even have radio. Someone riding by, playing a harmonica, could make a homesteader and his wife stand stock-still in the barn-yard till the last note was lost in the bazz-opp! of a nighthawk over the clearing. From that hunger, this story was born.

The first time I heard my mother play Mrs. Watson's piano, I almost forgot that Benny Watson had a .22 and I didn't . Even the men stopped talking and just stood there listening.

When Mother was finished, she smiled at Mrs. Watson. "Jane, that's a lovely gift from Becker."

Mrs. Watson kept looking at my mother as if she had never seen her before. "Liz, you must have had a career!" she exclaimed.

I remember my mother looking at my dad. Then she smiled wryly.

"Well, I thought of being a concert pianist. But I flopped. That's why I married Henry and escaped to this homestead."

"Lizzie was a great hand at the piano, I admit," Dad said. "But she found out that music ain't practical."

Ever so quietly, it seemed to me, my mother changed the subject.

It's more than 30 years now since those homesteaders gathered at Watsons' cabin that winter night. But the scene becomes vivid when I recall the winter that Benny Watson died. Somehow that wasn't as great a shock to my parents as when the word got out that Jane and Becker were selling out. Not to get away from memories of Benny, but because, suddenly, they never wanted to see each other again.

Their first two children had died at birth, and Benny had never been well. Even when his dad got him the .22, he never seemed to want to go out much with it. When he got pneumonia, he didn't last long.

Folks expected the Watsons to be cut up real bad. They said it was foolish for Jane and Becker to feel their lives were ended. They were only in their thirties, and well-off compared to most folks.

"I don't know who's more to blame," Dad said. "But it seems it started when Becker said Benny would be alive and well if Jane had taken proper care of him. From what I hear, they're not getting a divorce, just going their own ways."

Mother was shocked. "They're destroying themselves by their own stubbornness," she whispered.

"Yeah?" said my father uncomfortably, as he always did when my mother talked above his "Grade Four education," as he called it. "Well, Liz, we can't do nothing about it—"

"It's wrong, Henry!" Mother said, almost fiercely. "They'll regret it all their lives. But then it'll be too late—"

"Now, Lizzie," Dad said hastily, "it ain't like it was a sack of spuds they need. People's personal lives ain't our affairs—"

Mother didn't answer. What Dad called the "look" was in her eyes. They kind of look she'd get when my dad was feeling low, saying it was no use to clear a farm out of those stumps.

"I guess Becker will list his team of horses," Dad said.

"And his .22?" I asked.

"Stop it!" Mother's face was almost white. "Henry, sometimes pain can be a disease—and it needs outside help to cure it."

Dad just looked at me and shrugged his shoulders. I guess he still thought Mother was a dreamer—and maybe she was.

Next morning Mother baked a cake and announced she was going to Watsons'.

"And you're coming with me, Jamie," she said, "in case of bears."

"Lizzie, the bears ain't out of hibernation," Dad protested.

"You never can tell about those beasts," Mother said.

"I'm kinda scared of them myself, Mother," I said. "But if I had Benny's .22—" I caught my father's eye and shut up.

As we walked the three miles to their place, I thought about the piano.

Most people said Becker Watson was an idiot to spend his money on it, but when they first homesteaded, he did lots of things like that for his wife—especially after Benny was born.

I wondered if it was because of the piano that we visited the Watsons more than any of the other neighbours. It used to amaze me when not even Jane Watson could coax my mother to play it—sometimes for two or three visits. Yet when she did, her eyes would close, and her shoulders moved right and left with her fingers, as if the music had power to pull her body. Now if a person liked a piano that much, wouldn't she want to play it every chance she got?

Becker wasn't home when we got there. I guessed from the way Jane said it that he wasn't home much at all these days and she was just as glad. She tried to make small talk, thanking Mother for the cake and saying I was growing big.

But Mother said, "Jane, it's not for you and me to be talking like this. Is what I hear true?"

"I suppose it is," Jane said—as if it didn't really matter. "It's the best thing to do. This way we can start new lives somewhere else."

"You think you can find the future by going back into the unknown?" Mother asked slowly.

Jane gave her a strange look. "The unknown?"

"Whatever aimlessness you felt before you met and married Becker," Mother said sharply. "You have as much now as you had then—and more. You have shared memories, Jane."

Jane opened her mouth and looked at Mother, then started crying. She told how she had met Becker. How he'd always dreamed of a homestead in Alberta. How much they'd both wanted children. How he knew people laughed at them because they bought a piano and gave Benny everything—like that .22—when they should have been sinking money into the farm. Jane talked on about everything right up to the time Benny caught pneumonia, and Becker's blaming her for not caring for him properly.

"Jane, you've distorted everything with grief," Mother said. "You have everything to live for—if you're together—"

"No," Jane replied dully. "Something died. I can never forgive Becker for what he thinks. And he—he can never forgive me, because no matter what he says now, down inside he blames me for the loss of our boy."

Not a thing my mother said could change Jane.

One thing we did find out—it was too late to hold the sale that spring. There was the seeding and clearing to be done. And besides, there'd by no cash around until the fall crops.

But my mother did not like the looks of it. The Watsons went nowhere, and asked nobody to visit them. Mother kept after Dad to go see Becker and talk to him. Finally he gave in and went. But all they talked about was crops.

Going home, I asked Dad why Mother worried so much. "Maybe it's because she won't have a chance to play their piano," I said.

"Son, sometimes I think she regrets the years she wasted on music."

I remember that night still. Dad started talking again—as if for a minute he'd been caught in the spell of yesteryear. Listening to his voice, I could suddenly see Mother.

"Don't you fret about your mother, Jamie," Dad said. "She'll get over it in time—just like she got over her concert career."

Only she didn't. I sure knew that the August day we were picking raspberries. I was studying a raspberry, wondering about the little fine hairs, when suddenly my mother startled me.

"James Morrison! You're supposed to be helping gather something for the winter ahead of us!"

"I am!" I protested. "I'm picking as fast as my fingers can—"

"To stuff your stomach!" Suddenly there were tears in her eyes. "Let's go over to Watsons' right away, Jamie. You're all right—it's me that's wrong."

Jane came to the door—dull and beaten, looking almost as if she wished we hadn't come. After a little talk, she said, as if she was ashamed for sort of begging, "Liz, that piano. You know how people said Becker was silly to buy it for me? They say we won't get anything for it at a sale. I—I'm going back to my own people, so I don't care about the money. But Becker's going somewhere in eastern Canada—he doesn't know just where yet. He should have something for all the hard years he put in here."

"It was weird the way she talked," Mother told my father later. "Plain heartsick, Henry."

Mother sure fixed a supper for us that night—I even got two pieces of raspberry pie. When Dad was declaring it was the best meal he ever ate, Mother mentioned casually that it would be a great kindness to give the Watsons a fair price for their piano before the sale.

Father put down his fork slowly. I could see he wasn't enjoying his pie anymore.

"Lizzie, I haven't got that kind of money. Besides it'll go for a song at the sale. And besides, what about Becker's horses? And besides—"

"It isn't practical," Mother finished.

It was as if she had hit Dad. He just got up from the table and looked at her, then said, "Is that what you think, Elizabeth? I'm not planning for me, but for you—and especially for him. This is hard country. It'll take a lot of sacrifices and planning before life's easy."

"Yes, Henry, I know. I was wrong to ask. Buying that piano now isn't going to help Jane Watson, really. I guess I just don't know the right thing to do—and there's so little time."

"Lizzie—"

"Don't tell me it's not our worry," Mother said. "If we're to succeed here, we'll have to sacrifice in more ways than a man would think."

Then it was September. On the way to school I saw bills on the corner posts saying Watsons' sale was Saturday, November 10.

The Saturday before the sale, I figured I had better have it out with Dad about the gun.

"All right. Somebody will buy it. Guess it might as well be you. But only if it don't go over three dollars, mind." He pushed back his cap and looked at me. I'd never seen him look so haggard before. "Jamie," he said, "maybe your mother is right—what affects one of us here affects us all. Anyway, I wish the sale was over and done with. Meantime, Jamie, try not to vex your mother."

The morning of the sale, Dad hitched the wagon, and Mother climbed in, stiff and straight.

"How much shall I bid on the piano?" he asked.

"I didn't know you were thinking of buying it, Henry."

"Oh, it'll go cheap. You want it more than I want Becker's team. And with a bit of luck, we can buy both. You thought because I didn't buy it in the summer that I didn't want you to have it—"

"I don't want it now," Mother broke in. "I would have taken it before—to help them out—but not now. A bargain bought from people's sorrows is one thing I couldn't stand."

By the time we pulled into Watsons' yard, the women had gathered around the cabin, the men over by the barns, and the kids were running and yelling. I went with Dad to join the men.

Becker's machinery was lined up neatly on the south side of the barn. His four oxen were tied close to his team of horses.

I looked for the .22, but it wasn't with the machinery nor the harness, nor on the porch with the household goods.

Shortly before one o'clock the auctioneer arrived. He started on the furniture. At first, it seemed nobody could find his voice, but the auctioneer knew how to jolt them.

"Come on folks! Let's get started. These folks are leaving. Do you want them to have to set a match to their things?"

The sale began to go. A set of kitchen chairs. A table. Two oil lamps. Becker Watson, neither talking nor smiling, handed the articles one by one to the auctioneer.

Then Jane Watson came out, smiling at some of the neighbours. She did not look at Becker, nor he at her. But after awhile she couldn't keep her eyes off the things that she'd brought with her.

Suddenly Becker stooped over, then, as if it were awful heavy, handed the auctioneer a little cradle. Jane looked as if she could cry out; then a glazed look came over her face.

My mother turned her head away. I suddenly sensed she had been hoping something would stop the sale before it was forever too late. When the cradle went, I knew Mother admitted to herself that the last hope was gone.

"Now let's see those rifles, Becker."

I strained to see the .22, but it wasn't there. My father bought a .30-.30.

The auctioneer looked around. His eyes lighted on the piano. Right now was the time to sell this "impractical" object.

"Folks, here is a contraption that will turn the Alberta bushland into the kinds of homes you used to have. You all know this piano is the finest there is—and the only one we have up here. Who'll be lucky enough to take this home today?"

The auctioneer, searching wildly for inspiration, saw my mother.

"Mrs. Morrison! Will you show us how it's worked?"

My mother, always self-conscious in front of crowds, shook her head. Then suddenly I saw the "look" come into her eyes.

My father saw it, too. "Liz!" he whispered desperately.

But she was far enough away so she could claim she hadn't heard him. She sat down, closed her eyes and began to play. Slowly at first, then faster, her fingers moved over the keys.

She played some pieces I'd heard before and others I hadn't. The songs and hymns she'd sung to me when I'd had the flu. And those she'd hummed when Dad was feeling low, discouraged by the bush and stumps and frost. It was the music of all people everywhere: folk songs, school songs, and hymns my parents had sung before they came to the bushland.

I don't know how long Mother played—maybe a few minutes, maybe an hour—and I don't think anyone else knew either.

All I know is, I looked around and saw Becker and Jane Watson talking together in low urgent voices with their backs to the crowd. Then, suddenly, Jane hurried almost blindly into the cabin and Becker was speaking to the auctioneer.

The auctioneer nodded once, like a man who has seen everything.

Holding up his hands, he said, "Folks, we're neighbours, so I guess there's no need to explain too much. It just looks as though the folks here made a mistake about the sale. How would it be if those of you who bought just came up and got your money back? There'll be coffee and lunch, like always, and you can get a good bit of visiting in before the snows blow again."

The bush country, maybe because of its hardships, was one place where a thing like that could happen. Soon the men were laughing and shouting at each other; the women were exchanging talk and recipes; and the kids were chasing a squirrel. My mother was getting a few looks of awe, which she tried to ignore by helping Jane serve lunch.

I remember us waiting—dawdling is the word my father would have used—till the last team had pulled from the yard. Only then did Becker invite us into the house.

From a battered old trunk, he brought out Benny's .22 and held it toward me. "Would you like to have it, Jamie?"

I could hardly speak. "Well, if it isn't more than three dollars—"

"Money couldn't buy it." Watson's hands were trembling. "But I'm giving it to you."

He and Dad started talking about the land they would clear next spring. They'd help each other, and they'd use Becker's horses.

"Right now you can help us put up the stove again," Mother said to the men.

When we left, Jane and Becker were standing together in the door. They looked tired, but were smiling.

Suddenly I felt the first snowflake tickle the tip of my nose. The air was beginning to swirl. "Mother!" I yelled. "How many days till Christmas?"

I had rabbits to shoot and my part in the Christmas play to memorize. Mother had cranberry sauce to make and decorations for the rooms and letters to write to faraway friends.

And Dad hauled wheat to the railway. It seemed to me that he hauled a lot of wheat. But oxen were slow.

The day before Christmas I could sense something different about Dad. For one thing he insisted on driving Mother over to Watsons' to visit all afternoon. He had another load of grain to take to the elevator, he said.

"But Henry, Becker and Jane are coming over for dinner tomorrow!" Mother protested.

"I know," Dad said. "It's just there's an old bear that doesn't den up till after Christmas—and Jamie wanting to ride to town with me—"

That was the first I had heard about it. But I caught my father's look and figured if I wanted any more bullets for the .22, it would be okay if I went with him.

We took Mother to Watsons', then drove to the granary for the last load of wheat.

"Jamie," my father said, looking at the little heap left in one corner, "I done something that ain't very practical. All I hope is I ain't gonna start regrettin' it now."

But not till we drove to the station would he tell me what he meant. On the snow-crusted platform was a high wooden crate. For us! Dad got two men to ride out with us and help carry it into the living room. They uncrated a piano—bigger even than the Watsons'— so beautifully finished you could see your face in the wood! As soon as the men were gone, Dad got a cloth and started polishing it.

"Jamie, could I trust you to keep your mind off rabbits long enough to drive over and get your mother? Tell here I wanted to get the chores done early for Christmas Eve." He looked at me. "And, Son, don't say anything. It hasn't been too easy on your mother, and maybe this'll make up for a few things."

Dad met us at the kitchen door. While Mother was hanging up her coat, she was telling us how well Jane and Becker were getting along.

"Liz," Dad broke in, "do you remember that Christmas in Seattle? The time I fell in love with you—when you were playing at that kids' concert?"

Mother stopped talking and looked at him. Her cheeks coloured.

"Tell me something—honest?" Dad tapped on the woodbox. "Did you ever regret not being a great concert lady?"

My mother shook her head. Suddenly her face went soft. She went over to the archway where my dad was standing under a green bough of spruce. "You know I never did."

"Well, you never did tell me exactly why you quit," he persisted.

"I was too nervous in front of a crowd, Henry. And I wanted to make a home for you, dear." She looked into the living room and caught sight of the piano. "Henry!"

"It's for you," my dad said. "Come on in and—well—see if the frost has ruined it."

My mother started toward it, then suddenly she turned and came back, the tears rolling down her face.

"Oh, Henry, there were so many other things we really needed."

"Mebbe so , mebbe not. Depends on how you look at it. Anyhow, I wanted to do this for the best wife in the bushland." He looked at me. ''All right, Jamie, now go and shoot rabbits. When you come back, Mother will play some hymns for us.''

I looked at my mother, crying. Then I looked at my father and I shrugged my shoulders. But Dad didn't seem to see anything wrong. He put his arm around Mother and led her to the piano.

Watch at
the Window

This story has a history. When Donald Cameron (now Senator) convened the first Alberta Writers Conference in Banff in 1944, I was one of those receiving a scholarship to it. This story was read to the class. The late Georges Bugnet, a truly distinguished man of letters, was so moved by it that he and I became lifelong friends. When I visited him at the age of 100 years, he still referred to it. One wonders why it should have stuck that long in any man's mind.

Dad was getting the cows in for milking, limping slowly, not yelling at them the way he used to. When I passed him, after throwing hay and chop to the horses, he said his rheumatism was worse tonight.

I went inside the quiet log house—we still hadn't got us the lumber house Ma always dreamed of—and looked behind the flour sack that always stood in the small room adjoining the kitchen.

The pipe was still there, where Ma had hidden it ever since I could remember.

I no longer thought it odd that for most of her life my mother occasionally ''took a pull'' of the pipe, as she put it—a habit she'd picked up in Ireland from her brothers. I wondered what to do with her old pipe now.

Keep it—and learn that maybe it's the little things of life that bring you comfort? Destroy it—so Dad would never uncover the one secret she'd kept from him all through their marriage?

Uncertain, I went into the other room to look at Ma.

If it hadn't been for the simple coffin, you'd have thought she was sleeping after a hard day in the fields. Even so, she looked too little—too tired—for the life she'd had.

And not only because of the farm. Maybe more because of the way Dad and I never really got along. It can be like that with only two men on a place. The old one wants things done his way. The young one thinks he's cut off from the world—and what difference did the bushland make in the plan of things anyway?

Do the daily things a body's meant to do. And you'll find out who you are. Do it for them that knows you and you'll find it's what life's about.

I'd never hear her voice again. I'd only hear the whisper in my heart.

The funeral was tomorrow.

Our quarter section of white poplar and tough willow had been home to her since she and father left Ireland. Even after those 30 years, there was still bush to clear and roots to pick from the breaking. Hailstorms still rolled up in the thunder-heat of summer. Frost still left the wheat heads waving too lightly in September.

"It's no life for anybody, least of all for a woman . . ."

No more would Dad say that and hear her laugh a little and tell us that the hard times gave something back to a body, so that the good times would be better still.

The Barred Rocks came up around the door, their red combs tipped over their eyes. They were quiet and seemed curious. She had always fed the chickens and each one knew her. They seemed to be looking into the house for her, as they talked and humped over the step to the garden.

Dad wouldn't have time for the garden now. The weeds would soon take it over. . . . He'd miss her to do so many things—like milking in the autumn, when he worked late into the chilly nights to bind the last of the barley before the snows came.

How had she stood it? I wondered. And again I thought of the pipe.

Cigarettes were not common in the Ireland of her girlhood. Women who smoked used pipes like the men. But always covertly, never letting it be known. Ma had carried the habit with her to the bushland. Seemed to me her pipe was the one consolation she'd clung to through all the hardships of all the years.

I was seven when I first found out Ma had the pipe—and it was something nobody else was ever to know about. She smoked it twice a day, mostly when Dad was in the fields. It became my trust to watch at the window—especially if she'd been helping all day in the fields. She'd get a "pull" while Dad slopped the pigs. The minute he turned the corner of the barn, swinging the froth-stained pails, I'd yell at her.

Unhurriedly, she'd empty the pipe into the old McClary range and put it back in its hiding place behind the flour sack.

I remembered when everything seemed to go all wrong on the farm—one year in particular: first hail, then frost got what was left of the crop, and one of our horses died from staggers—and for a whole day my dad just sat there, not speaking, and Ma slipping the pipe into the front of her dress and going out to the chicken house "for a pull." I'd still have to stand between the cabin and the hen house, keeping watch, till Ma came out, kind of contented, as if she'd conjured some wisdom from the pale blue smoke. She'd go in and talk to Dad and the next day they'd start in again as if things were bound to get better.

Same thing when Dad and I flared at each other—I guess as much over the frustration of never seeming to get anywhere as over being two males in too small a domain. Nothing upset Ma more than to see us fight. She'd go away by herself—only I knew what for—and then come back and speak softly to us, and somehow the tension would ease between us and we'd start working together again.

I was the one who bought her tobacco after school, from the egg money she saved. In winter—when Dad stayed indoors a lot because of the intense sub-zero cold snaps—I had to keep an especially sharp eye when he went to do the chores. If it was snowing a curtain between the cabin and barn, and the first I knew of his return was his stamping the snow off his boots at the lean-to, I'd have to think up something to distract him a minute while Ma hastily took the lid off the stove and pretended to be putting more wood in. The wood smoke killed the tobacco fumes. . . . But there were close calls.

Only once did I really fear for the pipe she'd brought from Ireland. It was one of the really hard years, and somehow she broke the stem. It was a rainy afternoon, and we were both trying to tie it up with string when Dad came in suddenly and stopped like a shot man in the doorway.

Ma's face went white. But it was me whom Dad pounced on. "Where'd you get that?"

"All the kids have them at school. For blowing bubbles," I said.

Father saw the tobacco still in the bowl. "Can you not see through his lies?" he said to my mother. "Come out to the barn with me, boy!"

"Now be easy on him," my mother pleaded.

Fortunately, he left the pipe on the dresser—thinking he might use it himself if he broke what he called the "shank" of his own, I figured. As soon as we thought he had forgotten it, we fixed it up so it would draw again.

As I grew up, it was my money—earned from trapping a few weasels in winter or from helping a neighbour for a few days in the summer holidays—that kept Ma in tobacco. I'd have got her a new pipe, too. But she wouldn't have it. Maybe because thrift dies hard. Or maybe because that particular pipe, a link with the land of her birth and a way of life I would never know, was beyond any replacement. . . .

Standing there, I could hear Dad closing the barn door. For a moment, it was as if I was a little boy again, keeping watch at the window.

Put it away Ma—he's coming.

The words were a whisper in my heart.

Dad limped in slowly and lit the lamp. His hands shook a little.

"That's the worst my rheumatism's been for a long time," he said. Ma used to rub his shoulders with liniment.

I turned to start the cooking, wondering what to do with the pipe. Dad and I ate in silence. When the separating was done, we stood together by the coffin. This was our last night to be with her forever.

"I'll be glad when they put me beside her," Dad said.

It was as if there was rheumatism in his voice, too.

"And when things were kind of looking up, too."

Expression of his thoughts had always been difficult. All their years together seemed to be moving over his face. "She's the one kept this farm together. I could never give her anything. I think she thought—she thought it wouldn't matter, because somehow things would be better for you—"

I couldn't say anything. As if it was too much for him, Dad turned away and went out of the room to the kichen. He was back in a minute. He said:

"Do you think it would be all right—nobody would know—"

He had the pipe in his hand—the old pipe Ma brought from Ireland—the one she'd kept hidden behind the flour sack all those years.

Somehow, he'd guessed. Or he'd known. And he'd let her keep her secret to the end.

He slipped the pipe into the coffin beside her.

Then we looked at each other.

And for the first time, in all my adult years I think, there was understanding between us. An understanding stronger than words.

We looked for the last time at her.

And it seemed—seemed by the way the lamplight fell—seemed suddenly like Ma was smiling.

Big Mike

The central character of this story—an Irish immigrant to the bush country—was created as a composite of several I knew. The events were real ones from the depression era. This short story first appeared in the Family Herald *and brought such a volume of fan mail that the paper finally did a most unusual thing: it ran another story title on its front cover with the humbling blurb: "Another heartwarming story by Canada's best-loved writer." Exaggeration or not, it is the sort of accolade that is the writer's real reward.*

The shadow of the city editor fell across my desk. "I didn't expect you here today," his voice said, not half as gruff as it usually was.

I turned around and looked up at him. "I wanted to come—I wanted to do Big Mike's obituary my own way."

He looked doubtful. "He was a colourful Irishman—anyone who ever met Mike Collins had to say that. Just the same, it's hard to break form." He walked around the desk, thinking. "Was it a big funeral?"

"A mile long. They had a military parade, even—turns out he won some distinguished honours in France in the First World War. I didn't know that; he never talked much about the war."

"A lot of people are talking about him," the editor said. "Even people who scarcely knew him. Ran into Dr. Kamson today. He told me Big Mike was the strongest man in the whole hospital, orderlies and interns included. You wouldn't think they could build Irishmen like that on potatoes and fish."

"And sometimes little of that."

I got caught for a minute by the memories. Then I said: "It

wouldn't hurt to try the piece my way. Maybe it will give some other guy like him faith to hang on when things are blackest. Big Mike was like that. If you couldn't do anything much yourself, he used to say, you could always rally somebody else.''

The city editor lit a cigarette. ''All right—try it. Don't bother with the routine news of his death; we've got that—the major operation for the shrapnel that worked up and down his spine—that's hard to take when you're 71. Play up the time he saved the homesteads up there in the bush country—I'll send you the news clips from the morgue. . . .''

''No need—I remember. The depression was at its worst then.''

He looked surprised. ''You were just a kid . . .'' He broke off and nodded. ''Okay. Make it a good story.'' He went away.

It was hard to begin. I could see him there joshing with the interns just before the operation. Then that Friday morning three days later, when the relapse came. His wife, still living on the homestead, came by train. His four sons rushing back—one from as far away as Chicago. And Big Mike looking surprised—surprised and a little shaken—to find the great strength inside him stealing away. But not unhappy. That was never Big Mike's way. The leaves were turning russet and gold on the trees outside his window. He'd looked at them longingly; Big Mike had grown to love Canada in the autumn.

No—not that. That wasn't the place to start. Maybe with his wife. There'd been quite a few of the boys over, both from the papers and press services; and she'd asked me if I'd be the one who would write about his passing. I said I hoped I would. And she'd wanted to know, a little fearfully, what I'd put into it.

I said I'd like at last to tell the whole story about Big Mike—but there was a lot I didn't know, and she'd have to help. She stood a long time by the window, staring—staring across the years . . . and then she began to talk to me, telling me about the Irishman she knew.

Un-Irish people know of Ireland as a land of blarney and shamrocks; Mike Collins knew it as a place of toil and tears—but of moonlight and happiness, also. The world was different when he was a boy nearly three-quarters of a century ago, and Ireland was different, too.

Every morning when his father went out to whatever work he could get, Mike's mother would say: ''God go with you.'' It's a custom they still have in Ireland. Very early, Mike began tending goats on the hillsides for a penny a day. One of his greatest joys was to listen to the ancient stories of the *Seanachai*—the village storyteller. And there were other joys, woven around the fierce family love of the Celts, and the simple faith they have in God.

They were rich, even though the terrible fear of dispossession came over them. And young Mike understood it early—the bailiffs coming, their possessions tossed out on the street. Once he told me about it, his fair blue eyes troubled for the little barefoot boy he once had been. And then, those same blue eyes flashing with age-old wisdom and fierce Celtic pride: "But the joke was on them—for they couldn't dispossess us of our treasures. When my father found new work, my mother would say as he left: 'God be with you'." And when he returned at night, the door was closed against the damp bog air, and the turf was turned on the hearth, and there were riches in every heart. And if they were a bit hungry, sure that was nothing—for the *Seanachai* was still on the hill.

He was twenty-four—only a bit of a boy—when he first noticed Mary Ellen O'Reilly, with the black hair and the pride of kings in her walk—for the O'Reillys are descended of Irish royalty, they tell me—and despite the sudden fears of their elders, they were soon "talking together."

One night, when the white Irish moon made pearls on the hedges, Mike walked with her, wondering if he should say what was in his heart; wondering, also, if Mary Ellen was the girl he needed all his life. For the Irish love truly but once, and if one is lost, the other—like the wild geese—might never mate again.

But that night he talked of love, despite himself—for he was like the storytellers themselves—and Mary Ellen smiled at him, as if she had never heard such talk before and as if it didn't particularly interest her, anyway, at all—but for all that, she listened.

But something he must have said—when he was near desperate for words—made her turn to look at the strapping young man at her side. And then the smile stopped, for indeed she was wondering now if he wasn't indeed an impractical boy and too much of a talker.

When Mike left her at the door that night, he still hadn't made up his mind if she was the wife for him; and she still wasn't sure if he was the kind that would be able to get something permanent and support a wife. And there was that pause common to lovers the world over. And then she said, as he turned away:

"Well . . . God go with you."

And right then it was that Mike Collins knew. Mike was sure.

Naturally, his parents were not in favour of the marriage. Not that they were not as romantic and kind-hearted as any Irish people; but in Ireland, you don't marry till you have something or at least somewhere to provide for a family.

But Mike was old Irish, and he wouldn't listen. And though Mary Ellen demurred at first—for she was earning a bit that helped her own family, and there was the obligation to them to consider—Big Mike persuaded her to go with him to the storyteller's (on a night when the bogs were sheened with silver) and somehow, suddenly, she had no fears again. Without words even, she gave to Big Mike the treasures no one could ever dispossess them of—faith and love and more—a lot more—that would endure as long as they lived.

They weren't easy years. Big Mike and his wife both went to work—she at the potato-picking, he on the Duke's estate. And when he left the stone house in the morning, Mary Ellen kissed him and said: "God go with you." And he said, "And you, wife." And he got along fine, for he could load more of the Duke's timber than any two men, till one day a bit of an argument—nothing to speak of—started over who was the best man in the north of Ireland.

Big Mike had laid four of them down when the Duke came running; and a bit regretfully, for he liked Big Mike, he let him go.

"You'd be an asset in the British Army," the Duke said—a remark that set Big Mike thinking.

That night he talked his thoughts out to Mary Ellen.

"If we could go to Canada or Australia, wife. . . ."

But there was no money for the passage over, no way of starting when they got there.

"What about the Army?" Big Mike said. "There's a shilling a day for me, and you'll be taken care of—you'll not want."

"You'll be killed!" Mary Ellen said, fear sharper than any other woman of any other race might know, in her heart. "And the years."

"I'll not be killed," Big Mike scoffed. And he talked and talked, and at the end he said, looking into her eyes: "For them, Mary Ellen—for the weans. . . ."

And so, the day he went away, Mary Ellen kept the tears back. And when he was marching away to the ship, she whispered the blessing that came down from St. Patrick: "God go with you, man of mine."

Big Mike went to the rugged Northwest Frontier of India, to the riots of Bengal; at the outbreak of World War I to the sand dunes of Iraq; and when the Turkish Army collapsed, to the trenches of France. It was in 1917 that he got the shrapnel while dragging his comrades back to safety and the war was over for him. They sent him to a military hospital and then home, to Ireland.

The first thing Big Mike showed his wife when he got home was the discharge papers the army had given him. "A soldier and a gentleman," the Commanding Officer had written. "A man not afraid to turn his hand to anything." And he had a letter from his chaplain: "Big Mike is a husband any woman might envy," the letter said. "Always you could find him doing one of two things—fighting as only the Irish fight, or asking God's mercy on those he might have killed or injured."

Ireland, happy though he was to be in it, wasn't for Big Mike now. It was too small, and there were no chances for the young ones and no way for a soldier who'd seen the world, to express himself. One day Big Mike went back to the old Duke's and sought him out and had a long talk with him about Canada—for the Duke had hunted there.

"Collins," said the Duke, "stay here and I'll make you the head forester on this estate—and your boys can come in when it's time— I'll put it in writing, with a mention of it in my will. It's a fine war record you had—I knew your old officer: used to shoot birds with him in Scotland. . . ."

But Big Mike would not listen. "It's my own land I want—a place no man can take from me. They tell me there's lots of work in Canada."

"Canada," said the Duke, "is a young man's country. It'll be too much for you, Collins—it'll kill you."

But Big Mike learned enough from him to know that a soldiers' immigration plan was under consideration by the British Government; that as a veteran, he would have top priority . . . and so they packed their trunk (one trunk it was, and none too big at that) and their riches they took in their hearts.

The Canadian northland—the bush country—the endless miles of scrub and hills and loneliness. That first night, in a log shack with the coal-oil lamp lit and coyotes howling in the timber flats, Mary Ellen Collins broke down and sobbed.

And then Big Mike gathered his family around his knee and began to talk to them, holding the weest on his knee and giving another his army medals (out of the trunk) to pull on a bit of string around the floor. And when he had done, the shadows were not so flitting, and the wood stove had caught and was warming the house. And Big Mike, like he might have spoken on unknown battlefields, spoke again.

"This is ours," he said. "And no man will take it from us. We'll clear the land and it'll grow bread to feed the hungry. We'll ask nothing for ourselves that we don't want for another, no matter what his race or creed; and when enough of us are doing it that way, there'll be hunger and war no more. We'll live as Irishmen should live in peace and joy and without fear, and if anyone says to the contrary, it's me he'll answer to. And you'll each fight to be somebody to be respected, to build love and freedom and faith into this part of the land . . . like I once went away to fight for this chance.''

In the middle of that night, Mary Ellen wakened Big Mike to tell him a a long-kept fear in her heart.

"I never did know," she whispered, "whether you were a practical man or not, and when you went to the army, there were many that told me it was because you were not stable."

"And now?" said Big Mike.

"Never again will I doubt," Mary Ellen said. "And it's ashamed I am for keeping this doubt all these years."

"Och, I sensed it all along," Big Mike said—gently. "Your mother told me when we first talked of marrying, Mary Ellen. Now go to sleep and don't be troubled by foolish things."

And an hour later he wakened her. "Them that was telling you all those things—what have they got to live for?" he asked her.

"Nothing," Mary Ellen said, and smiled in the darkness. "Now go back to sleep and don't be troubled by foolish things."

Big Mike, with the boys helping, went to work. Around Silver Springs, where a hardy breed settled, they talked of him. Of the logs he carried on his shoulders off the clearing. Of him staggering in at night, when it was too dark to work any longer, his face smeared with blood from the mosquitoes that infested the dew-wet grass. And his wife worked as hard—sitting up nights after long hours in the garden and the barn (milking and feeding), nursing back to health some frail calf or a couple of pigs—building, always building. That debt with the farm—what of that? Wheat was a dollar a bushel! One big crop or maybe two. . . .

The bush grew thinner and the pasture smaller; when Big Mike climbed on seeder or binder, it was with a "God bless us now as well as in the day of trouble"; the fields waved, lush with green; the harvests were bountiful; the kids shone at school; the hospitality of the Collins was talked of for miles, and Big Mike never put a lock on his doors. The payments on the place were nearly finished. And then . . . the depression came.

To Mary Ellen, it was like the end of dreams. To the boys, in university, it was as if, suddenly, the daylight had ended. Even Big Mike walked the fields he had cleared till the great courage in his heart came back. He called them together—his family—and what did he say to them?

"Maybe we've forgotten something—that it's a poor wealth that can be taken from you. All riches belong in the heart. We'll keep on, the way we should—and then the rewards will be richer still. Tim's going into medicine—he'll have to keep on—and may the Curse of Claddagh be on him if, when the blessings are on him, he turns away the sick from his door because they cannot pay. Kerry's to be the writer—maybe, son, you can study at home. . . ." Planning again, reviving their faith.

In the third year of the depression, Big Mike made the hardest decision of his life. More money still was needed to see Tim through college. Big Mike mortgaged the farm—even though it was difficult to get a mortgage then. I think even he was a little fearful the morning he started for Edmonton, to try. But his step straightened when, from the doorway, the tears in her eyes (more for what the farm meant to Mike than to her) Mary Ellen called:

"God go with you . . . and bring you safe home."

A year later, Big Mike's farm—along with most of the others' in the district—was up for sale. Not by mortgage companies (for the government had declared a moratorium on such debts) but by the municipality, for taxes.

Big Mike, for the first time in his life, was ready to quit. Then he gathered his family about him and told them of Ireland, of the long years of hopes and dreams, of all the unspoken heartaches from the day of his birth. And then suddenly in the middle of the discourse, Big Mike jumped up. He jumped to his feet, and the tears were streaming down his face.

"I know how to do it," he said. "I know how to save us all!"

That was what first brought Big Mike fame outside his own world. The newspapers eventually carried his ingenious idea all over North America. But it wasn't that easy.

With a delegation, Big Mike went to the municipal council and proposed that, in lieu of taxes, the farmers "work out" the debts on municipal roads, bridges and other public works. The council hesitated.

"What of those who have the cash to pay?" the reeve asked. "They'll object . . ."

"Let them work out their taxes, too," Big Mike said.

"You can't run forever on work," the reeve said. "You need some money . . ."

"You can run for a year or maybe two," Big Mike said. "Surely there'll be something, then?"

But they still objected. And then Big Mike got to his feet and squared his shoulders about him, and somebody else that was going to speak, sat down. Maybe the old soldier was in Mike's voice, and the spell of the *Seanachai* in his words, and the power of mystics in his being.

Next Monday morning, down blind-lines and dirt roads, the first farmers' road gangs were starting out. The foreman was Big Mike; and following him, as they might have followed a god in shining armour, were men of every nationality and faith, but with one thing in common: the dream of owning their own homes forevermore.

That was Big Mike. His romance, his struggle, the time he saved the homesteads. But there was so much more—so much that was easier to envision than to tell: the stories he used to spin, the laughter he wooed from weary hearts, the faith he gave back to all who knew him.

When this operation had to be, he was not downhearted. I saw him the night before . . . helping the helpless veterans to get to their places for a movie that was being shown in the hospital. While it was on—for, as he himself said, he was never much "for the pictures"—we sat and talked.

"Many a man might sorrow over this," he said. "But all I can think of is that the shrapnel never moved into a bad position till *now*. It could have done it any time at all in the past 30 years, but it never came till I wasn't needed any longer. A man has much to be thankful for.

"And look at her," he said, meaning Mary Ellen. "She's never wanted. It's glad she is, I'll warrant, that she took the road with me that day. And Timmy—Dr. Kamson himself it was that told me he was too brilliant to stay here, that for humanity's sake he had to go on. And one of you a journalist—to be in a position where you can tell the people the truths that will keep them free. Aye, we kept the riches no money can buy and no tyranny can take away—and we added to them till my cup can hold no more."

The tears came into his eyes then—the tears of the terribly strong. Because that was Big Mike—a rich man among paupers, a king among commoners, a man.

It was finished, that obituary I was writing. But it was not complete.

I looked up, and the city editor was back beside my desk. I think he had been reading the sheets of copy as they rolled out of my typewriter.

"The end?" he said.

"Yes." I lit a cigarette, terribly tired, terribly weary.

"Well," he said, "well, it's not bad copy. I think we'll run this on the first page."

The front page! It was the first time for me. The city editor smiled as much as I'd ever seen him smile—a bare twist of his lips. "Maybe," he said, "you'll make a journalist some day."

Big Mike had believed I would. I think maybe I was his favourite son—he said I had the storytellers' art. That's why I wanted to do it—for him.

The city editor went away and I put on my coat. I thought suddenly, through tight shining tears, of the one scene I couldn't bring myself to write.

It was when Mother looked down at the coffin for the last time, and, in a voice I could scarcely hear, whispered for the last time.

"God go with you. . . ."

Pain
Killer

Here's a story with a history, too. I conceived the notion of doing a book about the characters in this story, but with a wife and young family didn't have quite enough money to pull it off without help. I applied to Canada Council for a $400 grant (that was another era, too!) but either I was too self-conscious to do a good selling job, or they really were out of funds. So the book became a series of short stories—and the very first one was published in Collier's.

Plowing in the Alberta bush country gave you time to worry without being disturbed. I needed it that spring—I had so many worries I could classify them.

Around the house, I worried about Pa and the homestead. In the fields, I kept worrying about how far Jay Cramer—our neighbour across the line-fence—would get ahead of us this year. Jay always managed to get ahead of us in everything, something that infuriated Father more than all the other troubles of homesteading together.

The rest of the time, I worried about Mr. Wrycjoski's daughter, Rose. I never suspected a man like Mr. Wrycjoski could possibly have a daughter as wonderful as Rose, till she came up from Saskatchewan where she'd been looking after her grandmother.

The first time I went out with Rose, all she could talk about was going back to Saskatchewan. The second visit, she said she was really getting to love the Alberta bush country. Somehow, by the time spring plowing started, we were talking about getting married and leaving our parents to look after themselves. It was hard to reason with Rose, especially when she had her arms around your neck and was talking a blue streak—but how in the world could a man look after a wife and nine kids (Rose thought that would be nice for a start) when I didn't even have a house to put them in?

Pa had promised me a share of the crop last year—till the frost came. Harder than clearing the dense bush and the endless work or even the death of your animals, it was to see your grain, one day waving high and heavy in the August heat, then suddenly white and lifeless in the wind. Since the frost, all Father could promise me was the utter ruination of our homesteading career if I didn't start using my head.

At the land's end again, I interrupted my worrying briefly to rise on the sulky plow and stand with my right foot on the trip (the trip catch was broken) while MacDuff, our best ox, jostled his three companions heavily onto the stubble.

"Stan-ley!" Faintly on the aimless wind, I heard my father calling from the barnyard. His voice sounded a bit hoarse, and I wondered if he'd been calling long.

"Stan-n-n—"

"All-l right! Coming!"

Unhitching the oxen for dinner, I suddenly noticed MacDuff "favouring" his left shoulder. When I edged my hand under the sweat pad, my fingers came out sticky with blood. Knowing Father, I suddenly acquired a new worry.

The oxen headed for the yard at a speed out of all ratio to the way they headed for the fields. We were in front of the barn in five minutes. My kid brothers took over. Bub was already hurrying to fill the mangers with musty greenfeed from the stack bottom. As Ed uncoupled them, each ox moved mechanically to the dusty wooden water trough, drank slowly, then found his right stall in the barn.

I went over to the old seeder, which Pa was repairing, wondering how he was feeling. Pa had been cooking four weeks already; and as Mother said, a man sees things differently when he has to eat his own cooking. In the days when Mother was well, Pa used to fascinate us with stories about his campfire cooking back on the Kansas plains. So when Mother got ill, Father was the unanimous choice for cook.

"You're sure getting the seeder into shape, Pa," I said cheerfully, wondering if MacDuff's shoulder would miraculously heal in an hour.

"Aw, the inferno with it!" said my father. "This old wreck was done five years ago, and your catching it on a fence post last spring didn't help it any. I planned on a new one this year, but having to buy seed grain sets a man back, Stanley. Much as I detest that crooked little Jay Cramer, do you see how smart he is? He didn't rush to sell his grain like all the other homesteaders. Not Cramer—he kept plenty back, knowing that some day the opportunity would come to get double the price. Stanley, much as I detest that little reprobate, I can't help but think you might do well to emulate him. There are always unforeseen opportunities for using your head to turn a dollar. But here you are, grown to man-size, and you haven't even filed a piece of land for yourself."

"Father," I said, "I think MacDuff's left shoulder is soft."

Pa crawled out from under the seeder. He gave me a look. He went to the barn, threw the harness off the big ox and critically examined MacDuff's left shoulder. Then he gave me another look.

"Stanley, did you or didn't you use the currycomb on him this morning?"

"Well, I think so, Pa. I think his sweat pad's too thin . . ."

"You think so?" he said. "What with?

"The good heaven above us and the inferno below us! You'd think a fellow come to your time of life would think about what he's doing. You'd think . . . Good heavens!" Pa said, "the dinner!"

Mother was up, taking a smoking frying pan off the stove. She looked white and thin in her nightgown.

"Nellie," roared my father, "what're you doing out of bed? I can do all the cooking needed around here. You won't be helping me any by causing me a funeral bill."

"A body gets tired lying, Sam," protested my mother, but she went obediently back to bed. After her operation in March, the doctor said her heart wasn't too strong; he ordered her to "lie four months." It was hard on Mother, knowing there was so much work to do.

I took her in a plate of dinner and heard Bub ask Father what something was. "That," I heard my father say, "is fried bacon. Eat it." Ed said enthusiastically it was like eating on the Kansas plains. Ed believed that flattery could relieve a person of many distasteful tasks in life, such as washing dishes when Mother was sick.

I helped Mother get propped up comfortably. I told her about a pair of mallards that were swimming in the upper slough and how warm it was outside. "The blackbirds are back, too. A flock of them follows the plow."

"Well," she said, "it's the 20th of April." Mother always knew when to expect the birds back. She never let Ed and Bub shoot crows, she was so glad to see them again after the long winter.

"The grass is greening—all the sloughs are real green. The poplars are getting catkins. There's bush fires up north; you can smell them on the wind."

"Alberta's lovely in spring," said my mother wistfully. "A body likes to be up enjoying it. Eat your dinner, Stanley, before it gets cold."

Father was worrying about the seeder again. "If we could get six new spouts for it, it would do another year, I think. But there's small sense talking about that."

Money, always scarce in the Alberta bushland, was non-existent that year. The homesteaders lived a life as tough as that of any pioneers; and sometimes it seemed incredible to me that once you got to the railhead, now only 13 miles from the valley, you could board the twice-weekly train and be in Edmonton in five hours.

Dinner finished, Dad pushed back his chair. "Bub . . . and Ed . . . do the dishes. Nellie, stay in bed. Stanley, get out and rub that beast's shoulder with painkiller."

The package we'd got the fall before had never been opened. It sat on the header above the barn door, along with bits of leather, rivets and harness buckles. On the outside of the box it said: "LOKUM'S PAINKILLER LINIMENT—The Standard Remedy for Over a Century. For Toothache, Neuralgia, Sore Back, Sprains, Rheumatism, Especially Good for Livestock. Not To Be Taken Internally."

Inside the box was a voluminous wrapper printed in eight languages. I started to read the English version, and suddenly my heart skipped a beat. Lokum's had a contest on. First prize was $100—cash. Second was $75. Third $40 . . . All you had to do to win was write a jingle about their painkiller and enclose one wrapper with each entry.

They had printed a sample of the kind of jingle that might win.

> *When from pain you need a rest,*
> *Lokum's Liniment is best.*

Prize-winning entries would be judged on their aptitude, originality and sincerity of thought. Jingles could not be more than ten lines. Closing date was May 1st.

"Father!" I ran out of the barn, waving the folder. "Father—"

Pa was just crawling under the seeder. He crawled out again.

"What the inferno have you done now?" he said. "Killed the ox?"

I explained about the contest and the necessity of getting my entry in immediately. "Just like you said, Pa—unforeseen opportunities always arise. We'll all think up jingles—"

"For the love of heaven," he said, "*will* you use your head? We're homesteaders—not jinglers."

"But, Father, I've got real talent for this sort of thing. It springs naturally from my appreciation of music. Remember in school—"

"Stanley," said my father, "would it be asking too much of you to acquire an appreciation of what you're doing? Now, get that ox rubbed. Put the sweat pad on him. Take half-furrows the rest of the day." He pushed his hands through the air. "I'd plow myself and leave you here, but you'd put the seeder up so the inventor himself couldn't make it run again.''

The oxen plodded down the field. Last year's stubble crisped in the afternoon sun. I thought about the prizes, the painkiller and Pa. Mostly I thought about what that $100 would do to Pa's opinion of my practicality. Lulled half-asleep by the squeak of the coulter, I soon had thought out a magnificent jingle.

> *Lokum's killed our ox's pain:*
> *And still he lives to plow again.*

By quitting time, though, it didn't seem quite so good. All through supper, all through chores, I thought about Lokum's. I even managed to carry on an intelligent conversation with Father, though once he said suspiciously that I was looking like a mesmerized rabbit. That night, after everyone else was asleep, I got up quietly and lit the coal-oil lamp. By the time the April sky was lighting to apple-green in the east, my best jingle was finished.

> *When Gramp was bothered with pain,*
> *He'd say 'twas a sure sign of rain.*
> *Now Lokum's each day*
> *Keeps his miseries away,*
> *And we've lost a fine weathervane.*

Easter holidays were over, and Monday morning Ed and Bub had to start back to school again. On the strength of my promise to buy fishhooks for Ed and a harmonica for Bub, they offered to mail the jingle for me. That night they trudged home, swinging their old lard lunchpails and looking extremely pessimistic. All the school kids, it appeared, were mailing jingles for their parents.

"Some of them," said my brothers, eyeing me as if I had betrayed them, "mailed ten."

By May 10, ducks were stretching lazily on every slough and the willows, green with leaf, leaned toward the still waters. The harrowing was done—miraculously without mishap—and Father opined it was time to be getting the wheat in on last year's breaking.

The great hope that had continued to beat in my heart till May 1 was gone. Twice weekly the mail was hauled to Wild Brier Valley, yet Bub and Ed had brought me no news. I was sure now I had sent the wrong jingle. I hadn't seen Rose for three weeks. Pa was taking soda for his stomach, the direct result, he said, of worrying about the mishaps I *might* get into. Ed and Bub were distinctly cool: from the kids living near the river, they had word that the first suckers were coming up to spawn. The sucker run always preceded that of the pike.

Suckers could be snared on the rapids, but you needed hooks to catch the powerful jackfish, schools of which stayed in the deep pools all year long.

Father had hooked up the seeder spouts with haywire, and we gingerly hauled it to the breaking. We filled it with wheat from the wagon box at one end of the field.

"Now, Stanley," said my father, "watch those brutes on the breaking. If the chains catch on a root or anything, this infernal thing'll fall apart. If I didn't have to milk, treat the rest of the grain, cook, do the heavy chores, look after your mother—" Father paused. "If you ever used your head, use it now."

The first day I almost went dizzy. There were 16 spouts, 16 disks and 16 chains that dragged over the seeded track. It was hard to keep watching them all at once.

The middle of the third day, the feeder bar stopped turning. I stopped the oxen. When he saw me at the granary door, Pa stopped shovelling the grain he was treating.

"Stanley, don't tell me. Let me guess."

"Father, I wish you wouldn't always be jumping to conclusions about me. The bar broke."

Pa staggered outside. He looked beat.

"Something's got to give here soon, and I'm afraid it's going to be my mind. Listen! If we're ever going to get this crop in, we'll both have to be free to get out on the land. Someone has to keep that seeder together. I dunno why I didn't think of it before, but what about Rose Wrycjoski?"

"Good heavens, Pa!" I protested, "I don't think she knows anything about seeders."

Father said patiently, "Couldn't she come down and cook for us for awhile—look after mother—slop the pigs—put in the garden— take care of the brooding hens—do a few little jobs like that?"

"Well, Pa, she's getting fed up with the farm as it is. She—"

"Don't blame the poor girl," said my father. "Stanley, that future father-in-law of yours is gonna be a hard man to live with. He thinks he suffered more than me last year just because he had more crop to lose. Tell him you'll lend a hand with the harvesting in exchange."

The next day Pa set out to visit the Olsen's eight miles west. Sam Olsen had once owned an old seeder like ours. Pa figured he might get the feeder bar from it. I walked the ten miles up to Wrycjoski's.

In the hollow below their house, Rose raced to meet me, her dark hair flying. She was just getting her arms linked around my neck when I caught sight of Mr. Wrycjoski surveying us from the brow of the hill. His red moustache struck straight out.

"Hmn," said Mr. Wrycjoski. "Flutterin', eh?"

"Papa!" Rose turned in fury. "Quit following me! Can't I even say hello to Stanley without you watching?"

"If I said hello to people like that," said Mr. Wrycjoski, "they would think I was a very funny fellow. Now I know why last Sunday you washed all the clean dishes and put away the dirty ones." Mr. Wrycjoski looked at me. "Stanley, you gonna marry Rosie?"

"Well—"

"Papa!" shrieked Rose. "You're driving me berserk!"

"Come into the house," invited Mr. Wrycjoski affably. "I want Mama to hear this."

Mrs. Wrycjoski was a thin woman, with a lined face and a kind heart. Mr. Wrycjoski mentioned to her that the trouble with their Rosie was that she was thinking about flutterin' instead of working. "When we were young, we got married first and then we fluttered, hey, Mama?"

Mrs. Wrycjoski smiled.

Mr. Wrycjoski eyed me speculatively, as I'd seen Pa eye some ox he'd got stuck with in one or another of the complex deals in which the homesteaders were always involved.

"I got 480 acres of land. Nice land. When I die, whoever marries Rosie gets it—all of it. My horses, too—"

"Papa!" wailed Rose.

"I don't feel so good these days, either," said Mr. Wrycjoski sadly. "Think of it Stanley. Everything I worked and slaved for—all yours."

"Stanley," wailed Rose, "he just wants you to come and live here, so you can help him with all his work. Don't you do it. Papa, why do you always say mean things to Stanley?"

"If he's gonna be your husband," said Mr. Wrycjoski, "can't I talk to him whatever way I like? Do I always gotta be polite, like he was just a neighbour?"

"Mr. Wrycjoski," I finally managed to explain, "I only want to borrow Rose for a couple of weeks, till we get the seeding done. With Mother laid up, Pa's in a state. Thanks Mr. Wrycjoski, for the offer, but if I have to worry about your troubles, too, I'll go stark berserk."

"All right!" said Mr. Wrycjoski sadly. "But I don't think you'll ever have a head for trading."

I stayed to early supper, lending Mr. Wrycjoski a hand with his chores. Then Rose and I walked down the range-line road to the valley. We talked about us. Rose said she was irrevocably against the idea of people having only one child, because the child was worked to death. "So, Stanley darling, just as soon as we're married—"

"But, Rose," I said haggardly, "where will we live?"

Rose was definite about that. It would be far away from our respective parents.

From the sides of the white dirt road, the dusk slipped wings around us. Last flocks of songbirds passed overhead against the mid-May moon, and their wingbeats were tiny thunder in the night. In her light dress, Rose was like a dream moving beside me, and the spell of the spring slipped over us again.

We dreamed. When we got married, we wouldn't waste our lives tending oxen and getting up twice nightly to keep the fire going in the chicken house (so the hens wouldn't freeze their combs). Our summers would be spent romancing. In the winter, we'd snuggle around the fire and talk. We decided to keep these sacred plans to ourselves.

It was ten o'clock when we got to our place. Father was soaking his feet in hot water. Mother was still awake. Rose went in and kissed her.

"I'm sorry you had to come to work for us, dear," my mother said softly. "It gets tiresome doing dishes, cooking—"

"Mrs. Harrison, I just love doing dishes and cooking," protested Rose. "Don't I, Stanley?"

"You're sweet, and so romantic." My mother dabbed at her eyes. "Like I was before I married Sam."

Father had managed to get the bar for the seeder, and we started afresh on Monday. On Wednesday, as we watered the weary oxen, Ed and Bub came racing madly from school. They had a letter for me from the Lokum Company.

I opened it with difficulty, conscious of Father's scrutiny, wondering what I'd ever do with $100 at this time of year.

"Pa, remember what I said about my musical abilities?"

"There's a catch somewhere," said Father, putting a match in his mouth and trying to strike a light with his pipe. "Hah! Catch them giving away money. Hah!"

The letter from the Lokum people said:

Dear Mr. Harrison:

An enthusiastic volume of entries in our Jingle Contest was received from your part of the country. Oddly, however, the judges found that two third-prize entries were also from the same area. The jingle submitted by yourself and Mr. J. Cramer were held to be equally appropriate, original and sincere tributes to the value of Lokum's Painkiller Liniment, famous since the War of 1812.

Therefore, rather than divide the prize money ($40) the judges decided to ask each of you to submit a tie-breaking jingle, to be postmarked no later than June 1, after which the final decision shall be made. . . .

"Well, that illiterate little sidewinder!" roared my father. "What right had he to enter the contest? He doesn't need the money. The man never bought a bottle of liniment in his life. Likely, he stole somebody else's box-top."

Father slapped me on the back. "Surely for an intelligent boy like you, it would be simple to do another? Eh, son?"

"Pa, they're not that simple."

The family looked on me suddenly as if I was about to inherit an estate, providing I could only prove I was entitled to it. Mother said the Lokum people must sell a powerful lot of liniment to give away money like that. Rose begged me to think of what it would mean to our children in years to come to know their father had got his start in life by something other than homesteading.

After supper, Father started to fill his pipe. There was no love lost between Jay Cramer and him, and the thought of $40 almost within our reach was, plainly, putting Father in a state.

"Be calm, everybody!" said Father, spilling tobacco crumbs all over the table. "For a change, I'm going to ask everyone around here to use their heads. A windfall like that could be the making of us here. If that Cramer gets it, I'll never rest in my grave." Then he looked at me. "Stanley, will you say a word to us on how to go about making jingles?"

"Well," I said vaguely, "first you have to be full of little songs. Then—well, the jingles just come."

"You hear that?" said my father. "Now we get full of little songs."

Father sat up till dawn, without a single rhyme coming to his mind. He was haggard all the next day on the seeder.

Rose was the first to produce what even looked like a tie-breaking effort. Rose had put her whole heart into it, and it was hard for me to tell her I didn't think it was what the Lokum people wanted, especially coming from a man. Rose's jingle went:

When my babies suffer and shake
Lokum's soothes their every ache.

Two more days passed, and the jingles got poorer. To aggravate matters, Father heard a rumour that Cramer had sent in a jingle the day after his letter came.

Father, on the point of panic, ordered me out of the field and into the house. "What did I send you to school for, if you can't make up another jingle? Use your head, son!"

I worked so hard that Rose was practically on the verge of tears suffering for me. Then Father conceived an idea. "Let's sing, all of us—Stanley's partial to good music. Maybe it'll help him.'' Father outlasted the others. For a whole day he sang an old army song, whose chorus went:

All around the wheel of fortune,
It goes round and wearies me.
Young men's words are very uncertain,
Sad experience teaches me.

It was no help. On Sunday, when the Wrycjoskis drove down to visit, I asked Rose's Dad what he used Lokum's for, hoping to gain a fresh idea for a jingle. ''Me?'' said Mr. Wrycjoski. ''For colds. I drink her overnight. My stomachaie-yie,'' said Mr. Wrycjoski, ''my stomach! But the cold—''

''Good heavens, Mr. Wrycjoski,'' I said, ''it's not to be taken internally. It says so on the bottle.''

Mr. Wrycjoski went inside and told his wife it was no wonder he wasn't feeling so well lately. He'd been poisoning himself for years.

By Monday noon, I was ready to give up. Sadly, with Rose weeping at my shoulder, I read the Lokum Company's letter for the last time. Fortune had been that close. And then, sheer inspiration hit me.

The jingle, finished, read:

Until the War of 1812,
Pain ruled the human realm.
Then Lokum's liniment emerged—
The Painkiller supreme!

Pa collapsed when I read it to him. ''Son,'' he whispered hoarsely, ''I knew if we all worked at it, we'd do it. That Jay Cramer never even heard of Napoleon or the War of 1812.''

''That was the war between Canada and the States.''

''Of course, of course,'' croaked my father. ''But when you look as far into politics as I have, Stanley, you'll see the Napoleonic influence behind it all.''

On June 6, when we were almost finished seeding the oats, Ed and Bub raced across the field waving another envelope. This time there was no doubt. Inside was a letter of praise from the Lokum people. Likewise a beautiful green cheque—$40!

''There you are, Stanley,'' said my father, his voice back to normal again. ''Now, the real test is upon you. Anyone can compose a jingle. Anyone can get hold of money. The big thing is, what are you going to do with this windfall?''

My father said, ''I want you to ask yourself what a successful man would do with that money. Would he invest it in a new seeder, at a time when the price of seeders is coming down? By the way, there's a good second-hand implement agency north on First Street in Edmonton. . . . Or would he," continued my father, "take $10 and file a quarter of land—next to his father's, so the two could work together— and save the rest for emergencies? I hear that the Smoltz boys have their eyes on that quarter west of us. Once they get a $10 bill in their hands—hah! Good-bye land."

Inside 24 hours, an amazing number of people dropped in to visit us—Ed and Bub told the school kids about my fame. Nearly everyone mentioned what a fine head for business I had. At my nod, I could have had a good bull, another ox or $40 worth of good spruce lumber that, said the seller, would be worth double the money by fall.

My father advised me not to rush. "Even better deals may present themselves, son. The thing is to wait. Act indifferent."

"But, Pa, I'm getting confused. I hate not buying things from people."

"Nonsense," he said. "They don't really expect you to buy. But they figure there's no harm in trying. Son, when will you tumble to these things? You won't always have your father to think for you."

That same night, Rose suggested we go for a walk. Walking, she thought we should get married, now we had the money to do it.

"But, Rose! You can't just do that. Wouldn't it be better to invest the money wisely, then maybe in the fall—"

"Maybe!" said Rose bitterly. "Young men's words sure are very uncertain."

It was the first time Rose and I had ever really quarrelled, and I almost wished the Lokum factory had got blown up in the War of 1812.

The next day, as we started seeding greenfeed, the right wheel on the seeder collapsed. Father said calmly he had better go west. He had noticed one wheel still attached to Olsen's old seeder.

"Meanwhile, Stanley," he said, "if you'd like to go to Edmonton and make a few speculations, I can manage here alone. We're early, anyway. I'm not going to ask you to carry with you a picture of this seeder—or to ask you to visualize what it'll be like trying to seed a crop with it next year if we get frozen out this year again. If the worst happens, we can always broadcast the seed and be back in the dark ages, as well as pitied by neighbours. It's your money. Spend it—wisely."

From the moment Pa mentioned I might go to Edmonton, I went into a kind of coma. I was hardly out of it when I came back on the Sunday night train. I had spent the money, every last cent of it, and only when I saw the stationmaster starting to unload express, did I fully realize that the miracle of being a man of money was over.

Ed and Bub met me. The Wrycjoskis had come down to visit, and it wasn't good manners for father to leave company. Mr. Wrycjoski had lent the boys his team of horses and wagon, so we'd get home sooner.

"Did you get my harmonica?" Bub asked.

"I wanted spoon hooks." This from Ed.

"What's this?" Bub's voice rose at sight of a square cardboard box the station agent was wheeling toward us. "That's a mighty small-looking seeder."

"It's not a seeder," I said, with both dignity and apprehension. "And don't ask questions till we get home."

With the horses it took only two hours. The sun was setting and robins were singing in the black poplars on Mother's side of the cabin. Mr. Wrycjoski and Father came out when Bunts, our dog, started barking. Mr. Wrycjoski appeared indifferent to the sense of excitement emanating from the boys. He examined his team critically, to see if we had galloped them.

My father watched in silence as the packages were unloaded. Without his asking, he knew the $40 was gone. And without the $40, I suddenly felt that Father and I were back on the same footing as before Lokum's recognized the worth of my jingles.

Mother was resting on the couch when I carried in the box. Bub and Ed took the smaller parcels. Rose and Mrs. Wrycjoski sat beside Mother. They had been talking a long time, for the coal-oil lamp wasn't lit.

Rose got up stiffly. "Stanley, I have kept some supper warm for you."

"No, no, Rose, later. I had a sandwich on the train."

I was too excited to eat just then, but there were certain formalities to undergo. I touched a match to the lamp and put the globe in place.

"Did you see much?" Mother asked.

I commented properly on the crowds, the store, the streetcars. "I stayed at the St. Louis Hotel—near the used machinery lot," I went on. "I looked over the seeders—"

"Did you buy one?" There was a ray of hope in Father's face. It had suddenly occurred to him that if I had, it would come by freight.

I shook my head. "They didn't look like much, Pa. What's the sense of buying a wreck?"

"What did you buy then?" From Rose—stiffly.

"Well, a Mr. Mike Finkelstein called me in to look over his store. I was getting a harmonica for Bub."

"The inferno below us!" whispered my father strickenly. "Stanley, you can tell us the details later. Show us what you wasted your money on.''

The first parcel I opened contained a sweat pad for MacDuff.

''For the love of heaven!'' whispered Father, aghast. ''What kind of fellow are you, Stanley?''

''Without MacDuff we'd never have got the money,'' I explained.

I went over to Rose and gave her a strand of dime-store pearls. ''They're not much, Rose,'' I said; and for the first time in my life, words came hard to me. ''But I wanted to show you I was glad you came down. And—and to show you that—''

''Kid,'' said Mr. Wrycjoski sadly, ''what good's them on a homestead? Girls nowadays, all they think of—''

''Be quiet, Papa,'' said Mrs. Wrycjoski.

Mr. Wrycjoski looked at her with his mouth open. ''Mama! What's she want them things for? Better something to wear—''

''Wear!'' Rose had put the pearls around her neck. She stood up, crying. ''That's the first present anyone ever gave me in my life. All I ever got was something to eat or wear—'' Rose fled from the room.

''Let her go,'' said my mother softly. ''A good cry always helps a body.''

''Stanley,'' said my father, in a martyr's voice, ''what's in that?'' He pointed to the cardboard box.

I opened it slowly. It was a phonograph, with two little doors that you opened, depending on whether you wanted the music loud or low. It was the first phonograph in Wild Brier Valley. I wet my lips.

''Mr. Finkelstein said a bit of music would lighten the loads up here.''

''Sure!'' said my father. ''It's a wonder he didn't tell you the cows would milk better if you played to them. Nellie, what in the inferno's the matter with you?''

My mother was crying. ''I haven't seen one since we left Kansas,'' she said. ''It—it brought back memories, that's all, Sam.''

''Mother,'' I said, ''I bought it mostly for you. With this, it won't take so long for the time to pass.''

I wound it up and put a record on—*Seeing Nellie Home*.

The music came out, stirring and wonderful. And with it, slowly at first, then stronger, something else seemed to flow into the room. The spruce logs faded, and the peeled beams across the ceiling, and the thoughts of next day's work . . . or last year's frost.

My kid brothers stood transfixed. Mr. Wrycjoski looked at his wife; the tears were streaming down her face, too. Only Pa stood in the middle of the floor, glaring at the phonograph as if it were Jay

Cramer.

But when the record was done, he moved unsteadily. He looked at Mother propped up on the couch. Then slowly, awkwardly, he went over and sat down beside her.

"Nellie," he said. "Remember the night in Kansas when I first met you? We were on a hayride, and coming home I sang that song for you."

I put on *Long, Long Trail A-Winding*. My father laughed at my mother and said, "Tell you something I've never let on about before. When I was over there in the war, and we sang that song, I could always see you Nellie. I always said to myself if I got out and got to you again . . ."

I opened the little brown doors wider and you couldn't hear the rest. I played *Old Black Joe, It's a Long Way to Tipperary, Wind That Shakes the Barley* and, especially for Mr. Wrycjoski's benefit, Chopin's *Polynaise*. Mr. Finkelstein said anyone with a drop of Polish blood in their veins would weep over that.

Neither Mr. nor Mrs. Wrycjoski were weeping. Mrs. Wrycjoski said, in a faint voice, they'd better get home, the pigs were still to be fed.

"Let them go hungry for once," said Mr. Wrycjoski. "And Stanley, instead of playing that da-da-da-dad stuff, play *Seeing Nellie Home* again."

My brothers wanted to play the phonograph then, and Pa got up from the couch and spoke to me in a low voice that couldn't be heard above the music.

"Stanley," my father said, "I reckon complaining gets to be a habit. But, son—it doesn't mean nothing when it's among those you love." He looked at the floor. "If you'd bought a seeder, it would have worn out. In the fall, I'll see you won't be forgotten, if you want a homestead or something. Sometimes, Stanley," said my father, "a fellow should realize he don't always need to use his head. Sometimes using your heart is better."

I went out to where my dark-eyed Rose stood silently at the kitchen window. She had her hands closed around the pearls at her throat.

"Rose?" I touched her sholder. "Rose, maybe the necklace isn't much. But some day—"

"Stanley!" Rose whirled around and raised her arms. "Oh, Stanley, don't ask me to explain! Just believe that as long as I live, I'll never tire of waiting for you. Now now."

It was a night to remember. We made a lunch and played the phonograph without ending. Even Ed and Bub were allowed to stay up. It was long past midnight when Mr. Wrycjoski finally hitched up his horses and he and his wife drive homeward. Rose would stay on with us for a few days longer.

Together, we stood outside, listening to the rattle of wagon wheels dying in the night, listening to her father's voice fading finally in the distance.

I was see-in' Nellie ho-oh-home,
I was seein' Nellie home:
Hurr-ee up, you stupid, silly horses,
I was seein' Nellie home . . .

The Washing Machine

I had just finished a three-and-a-half year stint as editor of a weekly paper, had just got married, had just sold my first major feature to the Star Weekly *of Toronto (for more money than reporters earned in two months then) and had just bought our first washing machine. Thanks to the fortune that favours freelance writers, an older man from the bush country came to our house, saw my wife and me admiring the machine and was moved to tell us the story of* their *first washing machine. I could hardly wait to get him out so I could get to my typewriter. This story is so much real life that practically nothing needed to be changed.*

Now that I am older, it all comes back to me in retrospect— the wonderful, stirring drama that every family can know, when things are tough and life is a never-ending adventure with surprises on every turn of the trail. I am thinking of the depression years in the bush country again, and the time my mother wanted a washing machine.

August was there with its sticky heat. The rich crops were beginning to ripen on last year's virgin breaking. The thick poplars of the pasture were heavy, green and lifeless. There was a lull for the men that always comes before cutting and threshing; and Dad was out in the workshop, tinkering around with an old gas engine he was trying to rebuild. He had his heart set on making it work, to save the hours of pumping by hand when the long day's work in the field was done. Pumping water from a depth of 160 feet in the ground is hard work.

Mother was washing the dinner dishes and staring wistfully out of the kitchen windows to the rolling hills. When the heat of the day eased a little, she would call us kids and together we'd wander to those hills to pick the ripe saskatoons that would be canned for the winter months. Mother was tired, too. She was thinking of the new life stirring under her heart. There were three of us to wash for now, and she had to work in the garden, tend the chickens and ducks and, too often, help in the field. If she had a washing machine, how wonderfully free her days would be. There'd even be time to enjoy that new baby. . . .

A car rolled up the dusty road—a battered, dilapidated old wreck, driven by a fellow selling washing machines. Mother recognized him at once, and her eyes lit up. But when he came to the door, she shook her head regretfully.

"We have no money."

It was the same old story the salesman had heard day in and day out. And he, too, was desperate.

"Look, Mrs. Bell, let me leave my machine here for 30 days. I'll come back then, and if you don't like it, it won't cost you anything. Maybe by then you'll be able to make a down payment."

It was an offer Mother could not resist. The salesman was hardly out of the yard until the washing machine was going—by hand—and there was no berry-picking for Mother that day. We kids went off to the hills alone (wondering when summer would be over and we could rest from our labours of berry-picking) and Mother washed everything that would wash. There was no labour to washing with a machine, she said. Dad came around from the workshop and smiled at her work, but Mother did not tell him of the dream in her heart.

She merely explained: "Since he wanted to leave it so badly, I thought I might as well get a bit of washing done! Gives a body a rest up for a spell." She didn't want to worry Dad by telling him how much she suddenly needed a washing machine, worse than she had ever needed anything.

And so the berry season went, and Mother added to her little pile of egg money. It didn't cost so much for a down payment. If she had enough saved when that salesman came back . . . and if there was any price for the grain . . . just enough over and to spare, so the payments could be met.

A fierce determination was born in Mother. She would have that washing machine, so that she would have more time to spend with her children, teaching them, guiding them, maybe even playing a bit with them. And she hit on an idea.

We kids would take saskatoons into town and sell them—a large water bucket full for fifty cents—and that way the kitty would grow in a hurry.

We boys were most resentful, but hopeful, too. It was bad enough boys picking saskatoons, but selling them in the village! But then, who would ever pay that much money for a pail of berries? If anybody showed signs of buying too many, we'd be so glum and silent about it that we wouldn't have many customers. After all, if the washing machine salesman could talk his head off and not make a sale, we shouldn't even have to make a second trip to town.

Unfortunately, from our point of view, no advertising agency could ever have decked us out better as saskatoon salesmen. We were burned brown by the sun. Saskatoon juice was smeared on our faces and teeth. There were saskatoon branches sticking in our hair. Housewives looked at our downcast faces and bought all the berries we could bring. There were no social barriers in our walks. In fact, I recall now our best customer was the wife of the local Mountie.

Fortunately for our morale, the sales course ended quickly. Mother had thought of the idea too late, for the berry season was done, and the wheat was ready for cutting.

But mother looked at her little pile of savings and felt sure there was enough there for the down payment on the washing machine. She was like a new woman around the house, reading the instructions and the literature which the salesman had left in abundance.

Dad was desperately anxious to get his pump engine going before he started binding. In the bush country, the wheat shelled easily and had to be cut at a certain stage and quickly. Dad knew he would have to cut from early morning until the heavy dew at night, and he dreaded coming home then to milk the cows, unharness and feed his horses, then pump by hand. So it was a great moment when we gathered around to watch him start the engine.

Dad cranked and cranked, and nothing happened. He choked the engine, and it spluttered once in blue smoke. There was a yell from us boys, but it was premature. The pump engine refused to go. Dad tinkered some more; it coughed and kicked and away!

The smile on Dad's face, as I remember, could only be compared to the dream in Mother's eyes when she first started the washing machine. Dad went out and rigged up a form near the pump. The engine was brought out and started. But alas! It would run by itself—but it didn't have enough power to pump the well.

Dad tried to hide his disappointment with a smile. "I guess I'll just have to wait, Moms," he said wistfully. "I was afraid there wasn't enough strength to it. If I had a new magneto. . . ."

He turned away, his shoulders getting more tired, it seemed; and I guess at that moment, Mother made the hardest sacrifice of her life. She stared at the house to where the washing machine was, and then laughed cheerfully at Dad.

"I've been saving a few cents," she said, as if very pleased with herself. "I just thought something like this would happen, and it ought to pay for what you want."

Dad was wordless. It never dawned on us, for Mother kept her secret hopes to herself. He just looked at us kids and said, "Boys, I want you always to remember what a wonderful mother you have— what a good and thoughtful mother." And that was all he could say.

But that night they drove to town and got the necessary parts for the gas engine. Dad rigged it up when he came home, tired though he was, and when the water started flowing into the old wooden horse trough, he just stood and stared mutely at it until the trough was full.

"Mother," he said, with the grand pride of possession, "isn't it wonderful what they've invented to lessen the load on a man's shoulders? This'll sure leave time to get things done now."

"It sure will," Mother said, glad because he was glad.

The next day the washing machine salesman came back. Mother explained to him that they could not afford a down payment, so he would just have to take it back. The salesman was just as regretful. He dug into his battered case and drew out another batch of advertising.

"You read this," he said, "and I'll come around after threshing again."

Mother took the literature gladly because I think she felt that as long as she could visualize and dream over the washing machine, it might yet become a reality. When she opened the new literature, a picture of a beautiful power washer—operated by a gasoline engine— stared her in the face. She went out and asked Dad how he thought the wheat would go, and did the price look any better? And then she went in and calculated what bills there were to pay and what could be expected from the crops; and when she was done, the dream was in her eyes again.

September came, in folds of russet and waves of gold. Dad repaired the binder, and we kids followed in the bullwheel track, watching the wheat sheaves get kicked out onto the carrier. Behind us, Mother, in a pair of patched and faded overalls, started stooking. Once the bundles were in the stook, at least most of the danger was past; and every bundle in the stook meant the washing machine was that much closer.

For two days, harvesting went beautifully. Then a canvas tore; and precious hours were lost, while Mother stitched it together and Dad riveted the slats back on. Once again the binder was curving and humming about the field, and the rich grain went up the canvases.

Then—disaster struck. The days were terribly hot. The world was a landscape of yellow—yellow leaves on a yellow earth, the sun burning hot in a yellow sky. Wonderful harvest weather. But too hot.

That evening, a breath of wind came out of the pasture bush, and clouds looped themselves around the timberline. The air chilled; and sometime in the night it began to rain.

Mother rose that night and listened to the rain beating on the roof of our prairie shack, and the prayer in her heart was that it would only be a shower that would dry in a few hours' time. As if for comfort, she took up the washing machine data from her sewing rack and began to read. And the rain pelted heavier on the hard dry earth, and each of us was awake, more conscious of the rain than if it had been pelting down at Christmas.

For three days it rained. The farmers tried to busy themselves in their workshops, hoping that when they came out, the September sun would be shining brightly again. They were worried now that the grain would start to sprout in the sheaves.

On the fourth day, a bright wind rose with the morning light, and the air was fresh and clear. Dad surveyed the fields steaming slightly in the September air, and his eyes were glad.

"A few hours of that wind," he said, "and we'll be cutting again."

The wind, as if determined to be contrary, rose higher; and by noon it was a gale lashing the wheat fields. The heavy stalks broke under the weight of wheat. Shelling set in.

I think it was then that Mother knew her dreams of a washing machine must be set aside. She stooked grain a little more slowly now, and she got Dad to mend the old scrub board. In recompense, she used water generously now; she could go out to the well with a pail and watch Dad's old engine bringing the cold water up from the bowels of the earth; and the casual way she watched the engine working told us she knew we were making progress; we were getting somewhere and next year there might be a washing machine.

The dream within her never died, though. Until the threshing was done there was always hope that prices would be good, that the yield would be better than expected, that there would be a little money left over . . .

We kids were going to school when the threshing crew began the rounds of the various farmers. With the curious retrospect of youth, we looked back on berry-picking as a glorious idyl, hoping with a kind of fatalistic despair that there would be some extra chores for us to do on the day the thresher came to our farm. But our hopes were in vain. Dad was a great believer in our getting an education, and to school we had to go.

Threshing lasted about a day with us, and the return was not so good. The high wind had shelled a lot of the grain. The rain had worked havoc with the rest, and the verdict of the experienced old farmers was that the wheat would ''go'' Number Three, instead of Number One Northern. The depression was at its grimmest, too, and with the harvest flow of wheat, the price dropped another few cents a bushel.

By lamplight, Dad and Mother calculated the results of their year's work. When they were done, Dad looked at Mother and said heavily:

''Actually it hasn't even paid to raise wheat.''

That night, Mother took the leaflets and folders she had pored over so long and threw them in the coal scuttle downstairs, where they would come in handy for lighting the fires in the furnace. She said nothing to Dad about the washing machine; he had enough worries as it was.

The days grew crisper and the nights colder. Dad plowed the stubble fields, and we kids picked hazelnuts along the line-fence and watched the geese going south again in long wedges. Mother, heavier with the new life within her, painted indoors and helped get out the garden.

The first night that it grew really chilly, Dad went downstairs to light the furnace. His eyes fell on the washing machine folders lying in the coal bucket. He saw Mother's thumb marks and her little notations. And then it dawned on him how much the machine had meant to Mother and how much she had dreamed of owning one.

The next day the pump engine stopped and Dad announced he had to take it to town. There were also two of the hogs old enough for shipping, he thought, though even to the practised eye of us kids, they were a bit on the light side.

It was dusk when Dad came home, and the blue haze of Indian summer smoked the countryside. Mother was upstairs resting, and so quietly did Dad come into the yard that she never even awakened.

When she came downstairs, Dad took her into the living room— and there in the middle of the room, white and shining was a new power washing machine.

Mother looked at it and rubbed her eyes, and then she just sat quietly down on the worn couch and started to cry. Dad told us boys to go out and see if the horses had enough feed for the night, and then he went over to her.

What he said, I don't know, but I can imagine. He would explain to her that it wasn't profitable to feed too many hogs; and when she asked about the pump engine, he would explain that it was too old to last much longer anyway, and better that he sell it before he was caught with it on his hands. Besides, next year there'd be a good crop and good prices, and he could get a real engine that would do chopping and cut firewood, as well as pump the water.

That night they sat in the living room long after we kids went to bed, where Mother could keep her eye on the new washing machine as Dad had watched his pump engine work. They could talk over the progress they had made and the life they hoped we kids would enjoy.

Or maybe they didn't talk at all, their hearts too full of understanding.

I wouldn't know. But I do know that in the hardest times of our lives my parents were richer than many people ever are, because they knew how to take richness out of sacrifice for each other.

The Kittlings

People often wonder whether a story is "real life" or "made up." Usually it's real life made up to suit the author's tastes! This story, set about the middle of the great depression, is real life—in fact, I originally intended it to be a feature. It came out under the fiction label, though—and perversely, drew more warm response from readers than stories on which I laboured both long and lovingly.

Just as some men are purebred chicken fanciers and others have a shrewd eye for good horseflesh, my father had a talent for buying, trading or otherwise getting stuck with the most temperamental, bizarre and highly individualistic farm animals I have ever encountered.

Lured by reports of the freedom and fortune to be had in the Canadian West, he left Ireland for an Alberta homestead in 1926. By the middle of the great depression, he had acquired—in addition to a more fatalistic philosophy of life—a number of what I can only describe as, for want of a better word, eccentric animals.

One was a big-boned Jersey that would eat rhubarb—the only cow I ever heard of that would. Our best workhorse was a Clydesdale with tender feet—the only horse with tender feet I ever heard of, too. He was ideal for work in the fields but hated to walk down the black bushland roads to town.

My father even had an odd-coloured cat—somewhat the shade of a turtle shell. Possessing a great Irish brogue till the day he died, my father called her "Tortle."

It is of her I write, for while the other animals were providers and helpmates, Tortle was—well, different: one of the few amenities of life in a new land. She was something to take my father's mind off the stumps that were so hard to clear, the mosquitoes that boiled out of the moist slough grass in mid-summer, the hail that hung from brassy skies over the wheat crops, the prosperity that never did turn the range-line road up to our homestead door.

Father's original idea, when he first brought Tortle home, was to have a cat around the barn to catch mice. Unfortunately, Tortle hated to get her paws wet, muddy or cold. Consequently, she took first to sleeping on the old Jersey in the winter nights, then to riding around on the Jersey's back. I need hardly remark that she was the only cat I ever saw riding a cow.

I believe that even in the animal world eccentrics attract other eccentrics and that Jersey was really eccentric. If you yelled at her, she would stop chewing her cud, gulp, then stand there, broken-hearted. She wouldn't let her milk down till her great cow heart had been reassured of human love once more. Moreover, because she had teats as thick as rope, we boys found her hard to milk in the beginning. She then became so used to my father's milking that she wouldn't let anyone else touch her udder. As old age crept up on her, she got even more temperamental: she wouldn't let go of her milk at all unless Tortle was purring on her back. Whenever milking time came, you would always see my father and Tortle heading for the barn together, Tortle with her tail up in the air, my father with a pail in his hand.

As if knowing how monotonous milking got for us boys, Tortle would, when her Jersey friend was stripped, spring lightly down onto the warm straw of the barn and sit approximately four feet from us, with open mouth.

This was our cue to try squirting milk into her mouth—a practice of which my frugal father heartily disapproved. When this got too dull, we would try to hit her in the eye or ear, which would cause Tortle to back up till she was practically wedged between the Clydesdale's hind feet. (The horse stalls were opposite the cow stalls in our slab-roofed pioneer barn.) Old Pat—the Clydesdale—would turn around to see what was hitting him in the fetlocks and for his inquisitiveness, often got a squirt of milk right in the eye. This made Old Pat as mad as a hatter, he would flatten his ears and shake his head as he burrowed into the manger, till the joy of greenfeed dispelled his irritation at being disturbed while eating.

Publicly, I don't like to say too much about this phase of growing up on a farm, especially since I am always telling the generation around me how seriously we took life with its grim responsibilities in those distant days. Back to the cats.

One day Tortle didn't show up for her evening siesta on the Jersey's back. In due course, we discovered she had five kittens, in a snug little hollow under the floor of the barn. This was bad—for Tortle.

"We have wasted more milk among them horses' legs," said my father, "than would've paid for this debt-ridden farm. I'm not going to have any more wasted. Them damned kittlings has gotta go. Frank, you drown them."

Frank, oldest of the three boys, protested as best he could. Then he went out to take a look at Tortle's family. He came back in and said he couldn't reach them under the floor of the barn. Anyway, he said, there was no rush. He'd do it as soon as they got their eyes open.

Tortle got so gaunt from feeding them that she would sit right behind us the moment we sat down to milk and hold her mouth open, mewing for milk.

"Dammit's soul," said my father, "can't you catch mice like other cats? What kind of cat are yez, anyway?"

Tortle would give him a little mew of politeness and open her mouth even wider. The performance annoyed, first, the Jersey who missed her old buddy the way a man misses his evening pipe; and, second, my father, who caught us trying to fatten Tortle up again, this time from a distance of several feet. He told Frank to drown the kittens as soon as we'd finished milking.

An hour after Jim and I took turns turning the separator, so we wouldn't have to watch Frank carrying the kittens down to the slough, I went outside. Frank was standing by the barn with a sack in his hand. He looked like the executioner. He beckoned me over. Being smaller, I knew what kind of beckon meant business. I went.

"You drown 'em," said Frank. "I have to paint the whiffletrees. And now, before the old man blows up."

I went in and looked at Tortle's kittens. They were the wildest-looking, cutest-looking little rascals you ever saw, about four inches long, all with little tails that stood straight up in the air like Momma's. Tortle rubbed against my leg to show her brood didn't really mean any offence the way they hissed and spat at me.

I went and got brother Jim. I handed him the sack.

"You drown those kittens," I said. "I gotta help Frank paint the whiffletrees. And right now."

Just before dusk, my father went out to see if the kittens were all "disposed of," as he put it, to my mother. Jim gave him the sack.

"You better drown 'em Dad," he said.

"Outta hell or ina hell," said my father, using his most exasperated Irish expression, "those boys are matchless. We've raised them to this time of life and they don't know how to drown five kittlings."

"Ye're best to do it yourself," said my mother. "The like of this nonsense I've never heard of."

She finally got father to concede he'd take care of it before going out to do the seeding the next morning.

The result was, we soon had five kittens lined up behind the horses' heels waiting patiently for milking time, when we boys would faithfully squirt milk into their mouths. Pat and the other horses, who raised their ears and snorted in wonderment when the little kittens first came mewing down among their feet, would turn around before moving position in the stall. And, by this time, the old Jersey had got so maternal about it, she would look around out of great purple eyes to make sure the whole clan was assembled.

"Hurry up, you old brute," my father would say. "Let your milk down."

The Jersey would give a great sigh, start chewing her cud and blowing like a porpoise, and the zing of fresh milk hitting tin milkpails must surely have been music to those cats' ears.

By fall, the five cats ringed around the milk stalls had increased to exactly twelve, seven of them stub-tailed and small. My father was desperate.

"Is a man to come to my time in life," he wailed to my mother, "and not have wan son that would lift a hand for him? I declare to God, them damned cats are bankrupting us."

Fortunately for my father—but unfortunately for the settlers south of us—that year was peculiar in more ways than one. For us, it was an exceptionally good growing year, especially where potatoes were concerned. The settlers to the south, however, got hit first by hail, then by frost, and many of them were forced to apply for relief.

Those days you could scarcely sell wheat, let alone potatoes. We had so many potatoes, we couldn't get a third of them into our cellar. My father let it be known that anyone hard up for potatoes could come to our place and load his wagon box.

So they came, most of them people we'd never seen before. My father would insist they fill the wagon box and then go inside for a cup of tea, or dinner, before starting the slow wagon trip home again—perhaps 16 or 20 miles deep in the range-line country to the south.

Just before they were ready to drive off, profuse in their thanks, my father would send us boys out to hitch up their teams. Then he would busy himself at the back of their wagons, making sure the sacks were well tied for the rough journey home.

Years later, I remember my father meeting some of those settlers and the great laugh that would erupt.

"Hey, Frank, you remember those spuds you gave me? Well, when I got home the old lady said they were movin'. We opened the bag and out jumped a cat. . . ."

Eleven cats jumped out in all—to eleven different homesteaders living in the bush.

"By gar, she was the funniest cat I ever see!" one fellow said to my father. "When I go to milk, she sit there like a dog, hees mout' open. I tell her: 'Go catch mouse. Don' sit there, making my cow nervous.' "

I can't be sure, but I suspect the cows got used to it.

A Memory of Gideon

I always felt this was one of those stories that should have been in anthologies and school readers, rather than the ones that were picked up. But maybe it was published too soon after the war. My own father was an old artilleryman, and the counterpart of the German artilleryman really lived. Both are dead now. And the events, of course, are taken from other incidents that happened to other people. . . .

For most people, Armistice Day may conjure up a nippy November morning, snow swirling around the Cenotaph, perhaps. For me, it will always bring back a June morning at Gideon School.

Carruthers was reviewing Geometry One, annoyed because the girls weren't paying proper attention, when the knock came on our senior room door. Ahead of me, Mary Kaminsky jumped.

Carruthers dropped the chalk in his pocket and strode to the back of the room, closing the door behind him. Moments later, he was back.

"Geraldine! Louise!"

The Korts girls rose as one, at the back of the Grade Seven row. They kept their eyes down as they walked quietly towards the door. The only time Carruthers called you out of the room was to strap you. Only this time he didn't have the strap.

Mary Kaminsky swung around in her seat. "Hey! What have *they* done?"

"Stick to your propositions, Kaminsky. Or the rest of us will be stuck on what you don't know for the rest of the week."

Mary stuck out her tongue.

I pulled her braids, as if they were horses' reins, so she had to face the front again. Carruthers had a habit of reappearing suddenly, hoping to catch someone out of line. For such minor misdemeanors as talking, he kept the senior girls half-an-hour after school. The boys got three hours extra homework. Mary never learned.

All this time, though, my mind was on the Korts kids. There was a fluttery feeling inside me, even before the sudden cry outside in the corridor—a broken cry as if, suddenly, nothing else in all the world mattered.

Geraldine. I knew.

Carruthers came back. His face was white.

"Carry on with the review work. You seniors all know departmentals start next Monday."

Gideon's population was exactly 85. The minute the noon bell rang, we filed sedately through the senior room door into the big hallway, with the cloakrooms on either end. Usually the half-dozen kids who lived in town took time off for a fast game of scrub. That day, they bolted.

They came back with the news that Pete Korts was dead. A heart attack. He'd been lugging stones off the summer fallow field by the blind-line road.

I listened to the buzz of voices, not quite believing. Every summer on the way to school, I had seen Pete hauling those stones, piling them around the fence posts. Seeding earlier on the sidehills. Binding when our own crops were still green in the hollows.

"Guess what? He asked if some of the Legion would be pallbearers!"

"The *Canadian* Legion?"

"What other Legion is there, dopehead?"

"I hear Old Lady Korts went running for your dad," Jordie Macdonald had sidled up to me. "Your old man drove him up to Adams'."

Mrs. Adams' Nursing Home was the best we had by way of a hospital back there in the Alberta bush. So I knew it had been my father who knocked on the classroom door. My father who had taken Geraldine and Louise home.

"So?" I said to Jordie.

He grinned. I knew that grin well.

Jordie was the first friend I had in Canada—from even before that morning our fathers marched us as far as May's Hill, pointed out the red brick of the Gideon schoolhouse, barely visible through the September-smeared softwoods, and told us to go the rest of the way together.

I skipped Grade 4, which left Jordie always a grade behind me.

Other than that, we had played together every summer, trapped the same creek bottoms in winter, and dealt each other more bloody noses than any other two boys in the bushland.

"You're stuck on Geraldine Korts," Jordie said.

"Look, Macdonald! If you tried a little harder, you could be almost as stupid as your old man."

"Okay, Irish—"

"Cut it out, you guys!" hissed Gershon Wetzel, the storekeeper's son. "Good afternoon, Mr. Carruthers!"

Carruthers could come around that schoolhouse corner without a sound. He glared suspiciously at us and, minutes later, rang the bell.

During noon hour, Mary Kaminsky had put a tack on my seat. Only four years under Carruthers kept me from leaping straight up in the aisle. Unobtrusively, I pulled down on both braids, till Mary seemed to be studying the schoolroom ceiling in mute, open-mouthed rapture.

Carruthers began with Grade Seven composition, leaving us with a sheaf of various old departmental exam papers. I looked, without really seeing. I was remembering things that had never seemed important before. Like the first time I had seen Pete Korts. . . .

It was a Saturday afternoon, late February and 20 below. Dad and I had hauled two loads of wheat; and as the team turned up the blind line, they galloped with the empty sleigh. The barn was only half-a-mile away.

In a thin black overcoat, the man hunched ahead of us, his face bent against the cutting cold. He had a parcel of groceries wedged under one arm.

He would have stepped into the drifts to let us pass, but my father shouted and pulled the team out of the frozen ruts of the road. When the loose snow hit their bellies, the horses leaped like crazy.

"Jump in, man!"

Pete Korts climbed stiffly over the sides of the sleigh box. A day's growth of black beard stood out against the white skin. His left eye twitched—shellshock, my dad explained later. It always twitched in cold weather, just like my dad's back hurt with old rheumatic pain.

"Danke!" Pete's voice was a growl. In the First World War, shrapnel had damaged his throat.

On the short ride, he talked little—partly because he was a quiet man, partly because he knew so few words of English. My father, who had been a gunner in the Royal Field Artillery, who had fought against, and beside, men of many races—in India, on the North-West Frontier, in Mesopotamia and France—had passed judgement by the time we let Pete off at the entrance to the old McCallum quarter.

"That new settler's a decent man," he told Big Jordie Macdonald, when they came up to visit on Sunday. "An old artilleryman like myself."

Jordie had enlisted with the Seaforths when he was 16. He had been shot through the right lung at 17. He rolled his eyes.

"The country'll soon be overrun with squareheads."

"Well, there's a few softheads here, too," said my father heatedly.

"Noo, noo," said Mrs. Macdonald. "Could you two no' agree to disagree for once?"

"Well, there's one certainty," said young Jordie's father. "Even a squarehead will never make a go of it on the McCallum place."

The following Saturday, when it was colder still, we overtook Pete at the cemetery, south of the school on the range-line road. He had a 98-lb. sack of flour over his shoulder.

"Dammit's soul," said my father, "you could borrow the team for something like that. They're standing in the barn all week, doing nothing."

I don't know whether Pete understood or not. He shook his head.

That day we found out he had been seven months in Canada. He worked in a coal mine near Edmonton, long enough to get the McCallum place, up for back taxes.

The McCallum place was so poor not even the Soldier Settlement Board would buy it when they were picking all the available land for soldier-settlers. But it was close to school, Pete said, as if that compensated for the stones and knolls and the waste of river bottom, where the horned owls hooted in the spruce stands in winter.

My father insisted on taking the flour into Pete's yard. The horses hated breaking trail. We had to beat our horsehide mitts together, to try to warm our hands.

"It's cold, Pete!" my father said, helping him shoulder the sack of flour.

"Iss goot!" Pete nodded. "*Kommen sie?*"

"Not today," my father said. You couldn't let horses stand out in 40 below.

But my dad didn't put them in the barn. He drove into our yard and backed them up to the woodpile. We hurried into the house to warm up for a minute.

Both airtight heaters were red-hot, the drafts at the front jingling like bells.

"We'll pick the split green poplar," my father said. "It throws more heat." To my mother, he explained: "No one man can buck firewood in this weather and get a day's wood ahead.''

When we drove the quarter-mile back to Korts', Pete turned from the sawhorse, rubbing an icicle from his nose. His face twisted by the cold, was a mixture of many emotions—suspicion, distrust, offended pride.

"*Nein*! No marks—dollars.''

"Dammit's soul, you can pay me back next winter,'' my father said. "Pete, in this country, two old artillerymen have to stick together.''

I didn't see Mrs. Korts that day, but I saw two little girls with long blonde hair, their faces against the single, frost-laced window-pane of McCallum's old bachelor cabin.

"I'll bring over a sack of spuds,'' said my father, "when the weather lets up a bit. They'd freeze in this.''

Pete, who had uttered not a word while we unloaded, shook his head, uncomprehending.

"Ah, so! Sputs!'' he said, when we came back a day or two later, with four sacks of potatoes in the back of the sleighbox.

We went into the cabin. Mrs. Korts, her hair in a bun, smiled and bowed at us. The two girls went into the bedroom. When we came out, it was blue dusk. The owls were hoot-hooting on the flats to the south.

Pete's face darkened. "*Eine horn-eule!* Not goot?''

"Oh, it's good when you hear the horned owls,'' my father told him. "Spring's coming!''

That March, one of the Grade Four girls went out to the cloakroom and told Miss Saunders—who had grades one to six—there were two little girls outside. Miss Saunders let them in.

There wore dresses so clean that my overalls suddenly looked dirty. I had never seen such long fine hair—like our ten acres of wheat, when the wind waved it in September. They stood side by side and smiled at Miss Saunders.

"Tell everybody your names,'' said Miss Saunders pleasantly.

The girls looked up at her and smiled again.

"Your names,'' said Miss Saunders.

The girls kept on smiling. The whole room began to snicker.

I put up my hand. "Miss Saunders, I think they're the Korts girls. They live across from us. They're German.''

Both girls turned towards my voice. They really smiled then. I felt myself getting red.

"Thank you, Patrick,'' said Miss Saunders. "Because you all laughed, there will be no story read today.''

She seated the girls in front of her desk. "They'll soon learn to speak English,'' she said.

They never said a single word—for weeks, it seemed to me. Then one day Geraldine jumped suddenly to her feet, when Miss Saunders was teaching long division to Grade Four.

She yelled one word. ''No!''

Then she sat down, smiling triumphantly. At me.

The whole room tittered. Jordie Macdonald pushed his pencil in my back. Miss Saunders went over to Geraldine.

''Very good, Geraldine. Can you say 'yes'?''

Geraldine shook her head. ''No.''

Carruthers, leaving the junior grades at last, chose the previous year's algebra departmental for us to work on. For correction, we passed our papers to the student behind.

Mary Kaminsky had a note in hers. Passing notes meant the strap for both—if detected. Mary's note said:

> *Stinky—I'll help you with art, if you'll help me with some stupid grammar.*

We returned the corrected papers. On Mary's note I had written.

> *You are too far gone for help. Besides, old C knows I can't paint.*

Anyway, art was not a departmental exam. We took it only once a week, for which I was grateful.

Mary pretended to drop her eraser. Reaching down for it—her face shielded from Carruthers' gimlet eye—she stuck out her tongue. With the toe of my running shoe—also hidden from Carruthers' vision—I nudged the eraser beyond her reach.

''All right!'' Carruthers came striding over, to collect the papers.

He studied the marks briefly, reviewed our weaknesses.

''Some of you are going to have to work hard this weekend, even to get 50. At any rate, you should know where to concentrate in algebra and geometry. Now we'll review English History. . . .''

I liked all history—but Canadian history was more real, especially the history of the depression years.

At first it didn't really matter that our house was only 20 by 20, so cold in winter, the water froze in the big crock in the kitchen and, in the summer nights, you couldn't sleep for the heat. Even Big Jordie joked about the ''Noah's Ark'' the S.S.B. had provided for him—a two-storey log building, built by the original homesteaders. Mice congregated in it; and the Macdonalds told us that weasels actually got in through the cracks in the logs to chase them. There was an average debt of $5,000 or more on each Soldier Settlement quarter, but we didn't worry about that.

"In another year, Frank," opined Big Jordie, "we'll be awa' sail-ing!"

That fall my dad threshed 2,000 bushels of wheat. We got 23¢ a bushel.

"You shouldna' have sold on a glutted market," Big Jordie said, rolling his eyes. "You should've held awhile."

Jordie sold his for 19¢ a bushel.

From then on, the interest on the debt was greater each year than the payments the soldier-settlers could make.

My father, being Irish, blamed the politicians. Jordie had a new explanation for the trouble—'them slave labour battalions they're kick-ing oot of Central Europe.''

He meant the Ukrainians and Russians taking homesteads on both sides of the range-line road in the heavy bush beyond the river. Their settlement, six miles south of Gideon, was called Skara. Big Jordie never referred to it by any other name than "the banana belt."

The new settlers were hailed out, then frozen out. My father gave them wagonloads of potatoes; we had so many that year, we had to store them in vine- and clay-covered pits in the fields, hoping we could sell them to one of the big hotels in Edmonton before freeze-up. We wrote letters, but only the Macdonald Hotel answered. They didn't want them.

That was the year I first saw the five Kaminsky kids. Mary, about my own age, looked so thin in her flour-sack dress, I thought she would blow away. She went to Skara school—a little yellow frame building buried in the balsam poplars.

For no explainable reason, Big Jordie was so wild over what my father did, he and my father almost came to blows.

"Ask one of them to build you a house out of them poplars"— Jordie's eyes were rolling—'and he'll ask ye a dollar a squared log!''

"Dammit's soul, be reasonable!" my father yelled back. "What am I going to do with them spuds? Let them freeze in the fields?"

Neither my mother nor Mrs. Macdonald said a word. They knew that, for them, there would never be a new home now.

Coming home from school, especially in the lassitude of a warm and bright October afternoon, even we kids would talk about the depression—at least Jordie and I and his sister Jean. The Korts girls would just walk with us, schoolbooks neatly under the right arm, lard-pail lunch box in their left hand, smiling every time you looked at them but not saying much—till the Macdonalds took leave of us at the blind-line corner and we turned west. Then they chattered a blue streak. My mother told me I was to let "the wee slips of things" walk with me. Nobody could convince her there mightn't be bears lurking in the tall twisted grasses that grew from the wet ditches—taller than the little kids going along it to school.

In a curious way, Louise and Geraldine didn't even exist for me then. Pete and my dad and I would work together, on jobs that one man—or even a man and a boy—could not manage alone. And on a winter's night, I would far rather listen to Pete and my father reminiscing about the war than play cards with the two giggling girls. Once in awhile they annoyed me—like when they would come to school on St. Patrick's Day, wearing home-made green shamrocks on their blouses, and Jordie Macdonald would ask me what part of Ireland they came from. In the summer I scarcely saw them, unless along the line-fence, picking raspberries with my mother and Mrs. Korts. In the fall, they would come over and help my mother make sauerkraut, which my dad thought was good for his rheumatism.

For me, the depression really became real the September I started Grade Seven without even new scribblers. Leo Agar, who ran the Gideon General Store, told everyone he couldn't "let out" anything more "on time." That was my first year under Carruthers who, for his welcoming speech, told the seven shivering Grade Seven students they were in the Senior Room now and at any time, whether he was out or in, he expected to be able to hear a pin drop. That same day he told me that no one could work without books and that every one of us was there to work.

For a few days, said my father—till the threshers came—could I make do with my old scribblers? "Maybe," he said, "I could explain to the master."

I begged him not to. If there was one thing Mr. Carruthers hated worse than not being able to hear a pin drop, it was parents interfering with his school.

That night, my father walked into Gideon. From the elevator agent, he borrowed enough money to buy my books.

The year I was 15, some of the soldier-settlers signed quit-claims. Les Agar went broke and Harry Wetzel, from Edmonton, bought out the General Store.

During the holidays, Geraldine Korts had suddenly grown tall—and saucier, too. (She called me "Patsy" when she wanted to make me mad.) The first batch of kids from the Banana Belt were coming to Gideon School—Mary Kaminsky among them. Now, Geraldine, Louise, Jean and Mary walked ahead along the range-line road. Jordie and I and a couple of the Banana Belt boys argued along behind.

That fall, Pete Korts, buying slabs up in the logging camps to the west, came across a small, broken-down sawmill, left behind in the bush. He bought it for $50. He and my father hauled it home.

"Life's damned funny, too," said my father.

He meant that Pete, who had started with nothing—but no debts, either—was better off than most. When he sold a bushel of wheat, at least the 40¢ was his own.

That winter my father's old rheumatism settled into almost crippling arthritis and Pete got a couple of men to help him with the mill— young, strong Germans just over, glad to work for their board. There were days the saw was silent in the old spruce. Somehow Pete got it running again. By spring, he had enough lumber to raise a new house and barn.

"Well, the poor devil earned it," my father said, as we watched the white rafters rise. "It would have killed ten men to fight with that old thing."

I had taken to trapping seriously then, saving back a bit of money each spring, for school books in the fall. And I knew what I had to do.

"Dad, maybe he'd let me work this coming winter? For lumber— enough to start our own home—"

"You're too young for that yet!"

The hurt in my dad's voice was not from the arthritis alone. I know that now.

That October, we got $1.19 for a 5-gallon can of cream. And on a night when the gas-lamp shone from Korts' new windows, through the thinning bush, I knocked on our old neighbour's new door.

"Come inside!" Pete's voice growled.

I went in, blinking against the bright light. Pete looked tired and too thin.

"Pat! Come in! Geraldine! Louise! Get a chair!"

Geraldine and Louise both brought a chair. Pete gave me the grimace that was, for him, a smile.

"How's Frank? That arthritis?"

I told him it was a little better; that he was starting to do chores again. And I told him why I had come.

Pete just nodded. "Ah, so! I was saying to the wife last night: this winter I need another man. When you can, you come."

"I can even miss some days of school—"

"Stay mit school!" Pete growled. "We got lots of time in the winter. Nothing better to do."

He looked at me again. His left eye was twitching almost all the time of late. "Pat, stay here."

He went into the bedroom—as big as our living room at home.

Memory of Gideon

When he came back, he held two old bills in his hand—old German banknotes. One, dated "Berlin, den 20, February, 1923" was for *Tin Tausend Mark*. The other, a beautiful purple, was bigger yet— *Hundertausend Mark*. I have them still.

"One time," Pete growled, "they would not buy a loaf of bread. I give them to you, Pat. Keep them. Iss good country, here. Sometimes when you are young, you do not know always what is goot and what is bad. Like we say in German: too soon old, too late schmart."

That spring, we hauled enough spruce to our farm to build the house that still stands there today. My father, helping us pile the last load where the warm Alberta winds would fast-dry the resin, said: "Pete, this is no boy's wages."

Pete growled. "I want to get the flats cleaned up, anyway. Make good hay meadows mit them spruce gone."

"I can't pay you, Pete," my father said. "And another dollar of debt would finish me."

"Iss paid, Frank," Pete said, and his voice was almost not a growl. "Long ago is paid."

"Pete, I'm hard up, but I'm not needing charity yet!"

"Ah, so! You think I can sell it, even at $10 a thousand? Or maybe so I should leave it for the ants?"

"Pete, this isn't a few sacks of spuds—"

"Frank," Pete said.

Almost hesitantly, he put one hand on my father's shoulder. There was the grimace of a smile again.

"Is not easy—I know. But—is not so?—old artillerymen should stick together. . . ."

Now he was gone. And there were two empty seats in the Grade Seven row. And Carruthers, finished with Grade Eight geography, was back— for a moment—at his desk.

Mary Kaminsky's fingers were scratching faintly on the outside of her desk. Another note. Carruthers was frowning over his timetable. I took it.

Shouldn't either you or me take the Korts' books home? Should I ask old C?

"Patrick," Carruthers said curtly, "I'll take that note."
I stood by the desk while he read it.
Slowly, the white left his face. Slowly the whole room relaxed.
"This once, go back to your seat."
I went.
"Yes, Mary," Carruthers said, more curtly still, "you may take

89

Louise and Geraldine their books. You will need Patrick to help you. Since they don't write departmentals, they don't have to come back to school. They will pass."

He paced across the front of the room—past the five rows of desks that marked Grades Seven to Eleven in Gideon School. He faced us seniors.

"Men of many races came here, to build a better way of life the only way it can be built—together. If you would study history, you would know they came for one reason—you. You, whatever you become, will be their only monument. And you will not even know it—because you are their monument to a dream."

He paced some more.

"Today, one of those men passed away. In the hour or so that he knew he had left to live, he made what will seem to some a strange request. He was once a soldier in the German Imperial Army. He hoped that some of his neighbours—against whom he once fought, and who fought against him—will carry him to rest. I know that one at least will. I have no doubt others will. What I hope is that some day some of you will understand why."

From the top of his desk, he took up our literature text, opened it. He came over to face us again.

"Who was Paul Brewsher? Mary?"

"A—a poet, sir?"

"Name one poem he wrote,"

" 'In Flanders Fields,' sir?"

"This is part of your English literature. If you don't review it, you can't expect to pass the departmentals. A Montreal doctor, John McCrae, wrote 'In Flanders Fields.' Patrick?"

" 'Nox Mortis,' sir."

"Yes," said Curruthers. " 'Nox Mortis.' It's Latin for what? Gershon?"

" 'Night of Death,' sir."

"That is correct. That poem reveals a pilot's thoughts as he flies with a load of bombs to drop on enemy cities by night during the Great War."

He replaced the book.

He went over to the east windows, his hands behind his back. As if to himself, he quoted the poem's closing lines:

"Oh, Star of Peace, rise swiftly in the East.
That from such slaying men may be released!"

Then he rang the dismissal bell.

◆◆◆◆

Self-Made Man

The pioneer way of life was rapidly disappearing by the mid-thirties—replaced by the hard times! After the Social Credit sweep of Alberta in 1935, one of the Edmonton papers carried an interview with a newly-appointed cabinet minister. I have always been haunted by one phrase in that story: "Referred to by those who know him as a self-made man. . . ." I started thinking about the self-made men I knew (are there such people?) and decided to do this story, which is a composite, I suspect, of all men who achieve success the hard way.

Interviewed immediately after the appointment of her husband, Frank Charles Grovers, to the provincial cabinet, a pleasantly-thrilled Mrs. Grovers admitted that the appointment came as a complete surprise to her.

She was alone now, for a few moments at least. She had taken the telephone off the hook, and she could read the papers over and over again. Late afternoon sunlight lay in a luxuriant pool on the richly polished living room floor. Right at this moment, Frank would be sitting in conference in his panelled office. He would be trying to look important, but in his heart, she knew, he would be impatient for the day to end, so he could get back to her, so they could exclaim together over the richness of their triumphs.

It was the struggle of achievement that made the prize worthwhile. Frank knew, after all these years. And she knew. *She knew!*

Mrs. Grovers is the former Mary Elizabeth Weyborn, daughter of pioneer settlers in Southern Alberta. She attended the same grade and high schools as her husband. "I fell in love with Frank the first time we met," she confessed laughingly, "so I guess you would say ours was a childhood romance."

He'd been a lonely, bitter boy then, almost a dreamer and mystic. The memories of her childhood came back to her in a rush. The old frame school in the middle of the prairies, the sun on the baked baseball diamond, the younger kids chasing yellow gophers in the dry parched grass.

They'd walked along the dusty dirt road to school, that morning, carrying their lunch. Frank was thin and undernourished—and silent.

"What are you thinking, Frank?" she'd dared to ask him.

And he told her finally: "I'm wishing I had an overcoat—like some of the town kids." And when she had not laughed, he'd explained to her, almost defiantly, the dream in his heart. "It's such a poor country here—dry, dry, dry! There's never any money for clothes. And when I take you to a show, my old windbreaker looks so shabby."

And she'd known. She told him she had; and when she saw the look of wonder in his eyes, her heart sang. Because now Frank knew. Knew she wasn't just a girl, but *his* girl.

She had chicken money at home, which she'd been saving for her first evening gown. A swishing, low-necked creation that would make him realize she was growing up. School for them would soon be done. There would not be the close associations afterwards. And it was so important that he remember.

She took the money one day and bought him a birthday present—a smart-cut tweed overcoat, not too heavy and not too light, so he could wear it nearly all year long.

And then she'd been frightened that his vanity might be wounded, that his pride might rebel because a woman had given him his heart's desire.

But it had not been that way. Tears had come into his eyes that night. And when they were done, he'd looked at her; and then suddenly he was a boy no longer. He was a man, and he was looking at her the way her heart had always wanted, and his husky voice was telling her: "Oh, Mary Elizabeth! Oh, Mary, my darling, I love you so. . . ."

The couple were married in 1930; and Mrs. Grovers saw plenty of moving throughout the province as her husband determined to find out, through experience, what his work should be.

They'd taken up farming that first year—in the flat prairie lands where the St. Mary's River died in shallow pools in summer, and you could look for 50 miles and see tall elevator box tops in a mirage against the sky. When they had crop failures two years in a row, Frank threw his hands up. All his youth had been darkened by drought, and his young heart could take it no longer.

"Some day they'll have irrigation here," he told Mary. "But I'm pulling out before I see this land kill you, too."

She wanted to plead with him. "Don't you know, darling, that a home is important to a woman—no matter how hard the life that goes with it?"

But she knew he had to find out for himself. Perhaps she had been unwise in hastening their marriage, that year when the bottom fell out of the world; but she'd loved him too much to let him go off riding the rods, footloose and alone.

She wouldn't complain now. Home was where her heart was, where her husband worked. On lonely cattle ranches, where the wind swept through the flimsy old bunkhouses. In one-room tenements in the city, while Frank broke his heart walking the pavement from day to day, trying to sell insurance.

There were little details about those days she'd never forget. How she sold a few magazine subscriptions to make ends meet. How wonderful it was to get invited out for supper once. How Frank rushed home one afternoon, shaking and incoherent, and she'd thought his mind had given way.

"No, no, Mary!" he'd yelled at her. "Don't you see—I've sold one big policy!"

It had been a day of gratitude. But the commission hadn't lasted long. They were pinching again . . . taking city relief, finally. Mary had to go and apply for that. Frank didn't have the courage. There was that awful evening when he'd said, "Mary, if I had one more debt or worry in the world I'd go stark, raving mad."

That was the night she was going to tell him about their first baby coming. She left it until the morning. For a long time, Frank sat there, not saying anything, and then he came over and knelt at her feet and buried his face in her lap.

"Don't worry, darling," he whispered. "The breaks have got to come now."

There was thick joy inside her, thicker, sweeter than she had ever known. Then she told him casually:

"Frank, I had a letter from home yesterday. There's a little coal-dealer's business open in town—if we want to take it."

The mother of two sons and a daughter, Mrs. Grovers admits that she doesn't have much time for hobbies. "When you raise a family, your hobbies, for the most part, are confined to the home," Mrs. Grovers said. A professional dressmaker, Mrs. Grovers was engaged in sewing for several years. She is quite versatile with the needle.

These newspaper reporters had given them a very remarkable write-up! With three children to rear, she'd had to be very handy with the needle. What the report did not state was that she'd taken in washing and mending to augment the seasonal returns from their little business. There were nights when her eyes were so tired that she could hardly do another stitch; mornings that she could have screamed when she walked up to customers' doors for their washing.

And yet she had never been too weary to talk over business problems with her husband, to hint to him, in little ways, how he might cultivate some of the men who could help him get on. In that way, Frank got an implement agency, and there wasn't so much washing to be done any more.

With even small successes coming his way at last, Frank had been incredibly good to her. "Some day, darling, I'll give you everything your heart desires—"

"But, darling, I have what my heart desires!" Sometimes she thought that men could never be taught that it was other things that counted, not the material surroundings.

Even in Frank, she knew he realized that the business he was building wasn't the end to him, but a steppingstone to something else. It was then she gave him the clipping which discussed speculation on an irrigation project for their part of the province.

"I told you it would come some day," Frank said.

"But don't you realize?" Some vision of what was to come trembled in her heart. "They're only talking, Frank. If you could stir the people up here, make their case known to the authorities—think of what it might mean—would mean—to all the farm people here, to the kids such as you and I were once."

Somewhere a couple in love laughed. Their own children passed them, yelling and shrieking in the yard. Dear God, Mary thought, where has my youth gone? And then—I'm young yet. There's love in the night for me, for both of us.

It lasted only a minute. Very gently she turned to him. "Frank, try just one meeting. Perhaps a speech that will get across to them, make them understand that they, the people, are sovereign." And when he still hesitated, she added, "I'll help you with it, dear."

Frank Grovers has been described by those who know him well as a self-made man, ideally suited for the difficult post to which he has ascended. Just over three years ago, he began taking a prominent part in political affairs of a non-party nature. His first efforts served to bring to the public attention the crying need for irrigation in the southwestern part of the province.

Mary put the paper down, feeling a sudden weariness of heart. The joy and elation were gone; and in their place was an ache that throbbed like old pain. Their daughter, their beloved first-born, was going to the University of Alberta now. The two boys were doing well at school. They'd be home, ravenous as always, any minute now.

Yes . . . Frank had arrived. But what of her? Since that first day when she had sacrificed to make him happy with an overcoat, she had known that her destiny lay in guiding him. Now, he was there. He would no longer need that guidance.

Like a soldier suffering combat fatigue, she went to the window and put her head on her hands and wept silently, without effort.

There was a sound of a car rolling to a stop on the gravel before their home. She started, then remembered. With this appointment, too, a new car was included. Hastily she straightened her face.

When Frank came in and kissed her, she could see that he had taken his first day's duties seriously. And she could see that he, too, realized that there were no more steppingstones; that in serving the people he knew and loved, he could find lasting happiness.

They were in the living room. She sank down on the couch she had dreamed of. He stood at the end of it, and suddenly he put his arms around her shoulders.

"I told you, darling"—he was trying to be jocular—"that some day I would make good for you, that some day I would give you everything you wanted."

She tried to speak and couldn't. The clock ticking in the kitchen was a vast sound that belonged only to time. Frank's hand patted her roughly.

"I know, Mary, I know." His voice was rugged. "I feel the same way."

But did he? How could he know what she felt? Frank still couldn't believe that the goal had been reached; his mind still couldn't grasp the new world that had opened to him.

"We'll never be poor again, darling," he told her. "We've got a toehold now and—and—" his voice faltered, and he didn't go on.

Poor! What did he mean? In her eyes, they had never been poor— not before.

"Mary!" he whispered. "I'm so unworthy! Mary—" His eyes began to swim.

"Darling!" She was comforting him now, as if he was a little boy again. "I understand, Frank."

"Maybe you don't." His voice was controlled, though muffled, now. "Mary, I stayed in that office nearly an hour after everyone left this afternoon. And I wasn't thinking proud things. I was realizing, for the first time, I guess, just who I owe this to. It was you, Mary.''

"Frank!''

"I've got to talk, Mary. Listen to me, please. All my life, I've leaned on you. You've been more than wife to me, Mary—in more ways than I can ever tell. Every time I got somewhere, it was because of you.

"Now, Mary, I'm—well, I'm where I always wanted to be, I guess. This is the kind of work I want to do for the rest of my life.''

He paused again, and there was the sound of their children calling to their school chums. Frank raised his tired eyes to hers.

"Mary, I'm there—and I'm scared. I'm so unworthy, Mary. I know so little and I have so much responsibility. Most of my life has been a failure—''

Suddenly in her heart there was a singing such as she had never known before. It was as if all the pleasures and joys she had missed throughout the years had stored up for this one special day, to pour in bursts of happiness through her whole body.

She rose and smiled at him. ''Bless you for that, my darling husband,'' she thought. But aloud she said: ''That's a lot of nonsense, Mr. Grovers. And if you do not believe it, well, you might read a book I've got. It's the story of a man whose life was one series of failures, too. About all he ever knew were debts, bankruptcies and sorrows. His name was Lincoln.''

She added, as she went into the kitchen: ''And you'll be interested in the write-up about us in tonight's paper. It's called 'At Home With A Self-Made Man.' ''

◆◆◆◆

Especially Worthy

As the first generation of homesteaders matured, the young bushwhackers—sons and daughters of the pioneers—were starting to leave for university (and not that much later, for war). The sacrifices of parents were matched only by their fears of what they—often unable to write a decent letter—were losing to the strange world of higher education. This story was sent to my agent who, believing it to be a first-person real-life drama, sent it over to Reader's Digest. *Grace Naismith, a senior editor, was rapturous and set it in type for the June issue (graduation). The editor-in-chief was suddenly struck by the fact that it might be fiction! They wired me—and though I desperately needed the $2750 they were offering, I couldn't lie. It has been reprinted countless times, however, and I will always remember a Brother Osmund, at the University of Alberta, telling me: "Fiction? I've seen it a thousand times. . . ."*

It was something of a sensation in our part of the world the morning we went to Edmonton for my brother Jim's graduation. Jim was the first one from our part of the country ever to go to college—an event that was a thing of both pride and doubt to my father—and that was back in the days when the depression was at its worst and the Alberta bushland seemed to be the toughest place in the world to make a living.

There was still dew on the June roses as Dad drove to the station. My mother sat stiffly in the front seat of the buggy, and I had the sinking sensation that she was more scared than she'd ever been in her life before. That was saying something, for all her life Mother had been afraid of schoolteachers and even of refined visitors, and only because Dad refused to leave the last of his seeding did she consent to go to the city at all. My father wore his overalls tucked inside his knee-rubber boots, which were colourfully patched with red strips from an old inner tube. I had on my good cap, with tissue paper in the lining — and in my pocket was a whole dollar to spend on anything I liked.

The night before, Dad had slipped it to me in the barn, unbeknownst to Mother or my kid sisters. All I could do was gawk. "Where'd you get that?"

"I borrowed it from the storekeeper," my father said, "and you don't have to shout it from the rooftops." He looked around, to make sure no one was within hearing. "Nipper, I want you to look after Mother at the speaking in there. Take her up where there's a good seat. And if Jim gets too rushed to take her to supper—or something— you remind him, eh?

I knew what Dad meant. Sometimes I figured that was why he was always making fun of Jim's learning. Maybe Jim figured he wasn't one of us any more. Maybe he was ashamed of us—ashamed of the farm and all the hard work and the poorness. Sometimes I figured the way he studied maybe he had forgotten that when we were poorest of all, we had the most fun of all.

"You know tomorrow means a lot to your mother," Dad said. "It could break her heart, Nipper."

The way he was talking to Mother now, though, you'd never have thought he was worried.

"Well, old girl," he said, "be sure to take care of yourself in front of that grandeur."

My mother gave him a look. She never could tell when he was teasing.

"You might tell them," my dad went on, "that any brains he has he got from his old man."

My mother was so nervous she could hardly stand his talk. It was only a desperate hunger to share in Jim's day of glory that took her to Edmonton at all. In that shining world of his, so removed from the farm, she felt she did not belong and that somehow it was a sin even to intrude. Education, as Mother said, is a wonderful thing. But in her mind, the riches of it belonged only to great people who were especially clever, especially worthy.

"I suppose now," my father muttered, "he'll be too good to pick up a manure fork. . . ."

It was the kind of talk that could have precipitated another bitter battle between the two of them, and I was relieved, as we went over Sam Mead's hill, to hear the whistle blowing as the train left the village ten miles west of us.

Dad seldom used the buggy whip but he flourished it now, and the surprised team leaped down Mead's hill so fast that I almost fell backwards out of the buggy and horse hair flew all over my good suit.

At the station cream cans were stacked in the shade of the long stucco walls and the station agent had his long wagon piled high with egg crates. There were a few people clustered on the platform— neighbours who'd brought in cream or blacksmithing work. They all lifted their hat to my mother and asked Dad if he was going to the city, too.

"Nope," said my father, "can't take time off from seeding." The way he said it, you'd have thought money was of no consideration.

"What's this I hear about Jim giving some kind of speech?" Charlie Porter, the elevator agent, asked.

"Oh, you mean his 'valediction' address?" Father said. (He had spent half of one night trying to find out the meaning of the word.)

"What's he gonna do now he's educated?"

My father looked unconcerned. "Well, that's up to him. I wanted him to be able to do something more than shovel manure all his life."

I could tell my mother was scandalized by such talk from Dad, for in the first place he had been opposed to Jim's going to college at all and his favourite pastime, in winter, was to write letters to agricultural experts commending them on their various ideas for improving the farm and asking if they had any alternative plans, where you used haywire instead of cash.

There was no time for further talk, though, for the train was bearing down on us—a black, hissing monster that made the platform tremble as it passed.

It was my first train ride and I hoped it would last for days. After awhile, however, it grew a bit monotonous. I was tired of drinking water in little paper cups, tired of staring out of the windows at the sloughs, with their brown muskeg waters and wild ducks rising into the air as the train clattered by. In every little field, carved out of the shining green poplars and the grey scrub willow, farmers were seeding, standing erect behind the levers, as the old wooden drills raised dust clouds behind them.

Finally I went back and sat beside Mother. She had a seat by herself, so she wouldn't be obliged to talk to strangers. She was reading the invitation again, the little card with the green-and-gold crest that invited my parents to the graduation exercises in Convocation Hall and announced the valedictory address would be by James Hugh Kelly. That was Jim.

Suddenly it seemed to me a long time since Jim went away. For two years he'd hardly been home at all, except for the odd weekend. The summer before, he'd spent all the holidays freighting on the Mackenzie waterways. I could hardly remember what he looked like.

"Why didn't he help us on the farm, instead of working on a stern-wheeler?" I asked Mother.

"It was to earn the money to put him through," my mother said severely. "If you're ever going to be something, you have to have an education."

Somehow, in the way she said it I could sense her praying that she would conduct herself properly—that now that Jim was somebody, he wouldn't need to be ashamed because of his family.

It took about four hours to get to Edmonton. We went down the platform between dizzying lines of track, and I had never seen so many people in my life before. I was so busy gawking I lost sight of Mother, and a man's suitcase sent me sprawling.

"Watch where you're going!" Mother scolded me. "And look at your suit, we haven't money to be buying you clothes every year."

I was kind of thankful when Jim met us in the station itself. What I noticed most about him was his haircut and his pressed suit. He grabbed me, as if he didn't know whether just to shake hands or swing me up the way he used to in the old days.

"Well, Nipper!" he laughed. "You and your pants sure have a hard time staying the same size!"

Then he looked at Mother, and for a moment, before he kissed her, I thought I saw a worry in his eyes. He was looking at her vividly-coloured print dress that had been washed—by hand—too many times to look new.

Then he laughed again and took us to a café. We thought he'd have dinner with us, but it turned out he still hadn't got his speech right and he wanted to spend more time on it.

I could see the disappointment in Mother's eyes. Then, surreptitiously she fumbled with the catch of her old purse. "Here, Jim, you'll want a few cents to treat your friends afterwards."

"Aw, Mother—" I could see the bleakness back in Jim's eyes . . . as if, I thought suddenly, her money wasn't as good as other people's. But he took the two dollars she gave him, anyway, his face tight and different.

"I'll pay you back every cent," he said.

I wanted to say to him: "The only time you can ever pay her back, Jim, is right now." I wanted to desperately; but I was just too dumb to say anything. I knew at that minute Mother would have given everything just to have him eat with her for the last time before the mysterious evening ritual when he would pass forever from her hard world and become a man of learning. I could see the tears standing in her tired eyes as he walked away.

Mother and I ate alone. Then, for two hours, we trudged from one store to another, trying to pick a present for Jim. Nothing seemed practical enough for Mother, or else she couldn't afford it with the few dollars she had left. She priced a pair of slippers and turned away because they were too dear. The salesclerk gave a short, brittle laugh, and I felt embarassed because everybody could tell we were from the country and they were either amused or annoyed by us.

Finally we took a streetcar for the South Side, and we went back to shopping. Mother bought a 25-cent pipe for Dad, giving it a couple of experimental pulls to make sure the hole wasn't plugged up. She got some cloth to make dresses for the girls. Finally she bought Jim a striped shirt with a stiff collar, which cost more than all the other things together.

Jim had told us where we could get a room. It was near the University. It was hot and stuffy, and Mother let me take my coat off. She started fixing her hair with old-fashioned hairpins, all the while talking about how grand Jim had looked and how hard he had worked to be "something." I kicked my heels on the lumpy old bed and knew she was getting more scared, and this talk was only to bolster courage. I was getting scared too—I didn't know why.

There was a knock at the door that made me jump. The hotel manager told Mother she was wanted on the telephone. Plain as day I could hear Jim's voice at the other end. He was explaining to Mother that his speech still wasn't satisfactory . . . that we were to have supper alone . . . that he'd pick us up in time to get to Convocation Hall.

I don't know when I have ever spent a more miserable afternoon. I didn't even feel like going out and spending the dollar. It was as if I was in a strange land where everybody rushed, nobody knew anyone else—and nobody cared. I wished I was back snaring gophers in the school grounds, or riding on the dusty, screeching old seeder with Dad.

My mother talked over the days since Jim had gone away. "Many a time," she reflected, "I never knew where the money was coming from. But we got him through, thank God. Now he won't need me no more."

To her, I guess, those words were a triumph; they meant that, through her, Jim had got somewhere. But to me, they seemed the saddest words I had ever heard.

Convocation Hall took my breath away. The college colours— green and gold—were everywhere. The place was packed. The men all wore dark suits; the women had beautiful corsages. The great velvet curtains up on the stage were billowing softly, like something from a storybook. Dignified men—some fat and clean-shaven, some thin with little dark goatees, all of them preoccupied and seemingly oblivious of the soft buzzing of the crowd—disappeared towards the stage, reappeared again, walking soundlessly as if they didn't want to be seen and yet were quite conscious of the scrutiny.

"The profs," Jim said absently, when I asked who they were.

A couple of fellows about Jim's age came by, showing each other graduation gifts from "the folks." One had a gold watch and the other was waving a cheque, and both were laughing.

"I didn't know what to get ye," Mother said, in an aside to Jim. "So I bought you a shirt."

"Oh—yeah—thanks, Mother," Jim whispered back. "You should not have bothered."

Somehow I was glad I had made Mother leave the shirt in the hotel room. I told her Jim would have no place to put it while he was making the speech.

Now, as he led us to a seat in the shadows near the back, I wanted to tell him what Dad had said, only Mother would have heard. I was beginning to feel as if I had stolen the dollar.

Jim was a bit pale, smiling vacantly at people who spoke to him. Either he was looking for somebody—or else he didn't want anybody to know we were his people.

Mother was staring at the beautiful gowns and hairdos of the women next to her. Then she looked at their hands and buried her own below her handbag. Her fingers were twisted and bent from the hard years on the farm.

"Well—I have to go now!" Jim smiled shakily at us. "It'll start in a minute. I'll see you right afterwards."

He was a few feet away, and I hollered at him.

"Jim! Wait a minute!"

Jim stopped, and I felt as if everybody in the hall was staring in our direction.

"Don't be tormenting him now! And him with his speech to give!" Mother warned angrily. But she wasn't quick enough to get hold of me before I was out of the seat and darting down the aisle.

I didn't say anything more to Jim until we were outside. Even then, it seemed crazy what I was saying and I was scared Jim would be mad at me for the rest of his life. But I had to tell him.

"Jim," I said, "didn't you want us to come?"

The breath hissed through Jim's teeth. "You're crazy, kid!"

"No, I'm not," I said. "I thought this was going to be fun.

Mother looked forward so long for this—but you've forgotten."

"Forgotten what, Nipper?" Jim said, and his eyes looked as if he had a headache.

"The last time you needed money," I said. "Mother dug senega root in summer to get that. Every minute she wasn't doing her own work, she was out there digging. You've forgotten how hard it is to dig snake-root. The mosquitoes were so bad that when she'd come home, her clothes would be covered with blood."

"What are you trying to say, kid?" Jim seemed to yell at me, but it was only a whisper.

"She did it so you could have an education," I told him.

And all of a sudden, remembering her pleadings with Dad, remembering her keeping baby lambs in the kitchen all winter, going without eggs so she could sell them, getting headaches in the heat of August from picking berries to peddle to the townspeople—all of a sudden I could hardly see.

"I don't even know how Dad rustled the money so we could come," I said. "But I know he did it because he wanted her to have something for all she'd done. Jim, she doesn't know what to do or say—"

But I couldn't tell Jim any more.

I couldn't upset him on the biggest night of his life. That would have broken Mother's heart. The way he looked at me—like somebody who's known all along that what he was hearing was true, but that, maybe, if somebody didn't tell him he wouldn't have to face it—I was scared maybe I'd put his speech right out of his mind. I ran indoors and left him there.

There was a lot I missed, in between "O Canada" and the appearance of a distinguished-looking man, in formal black clothes, who bowed against the backdrop of the brilliantly-lighted stage. He spoke briefly of the events that had gone before, then said he would call on James Hugh Kelly, the university's outstanding honours scholar of the year, to deliver the valedictory address.

Off-stage in the wings, the band began to play softly, the haunting theme song of the college. Then Jim stepped lightly across the stage, to a tiny table with a water pitcher on it. The drums sounded a deep roll and died. Applause came from the packed auditorium. The lights were off, but I could see the tears slipping down my mother's cheeks. She was so proud of him that nothing could spoil that moment for her.

"He's something at last," she was thinking.

Jim opened his address, and I could tell he was nervous. He said none of us gathered there that night would ever forget the memorable occasion. For the students, Jim said, it was both an ending and a beginning. He talked about the student year and the Tuck Shop and there was laughter, and that seemed to relax him.

With a sort of easy confidence now, he talked; and it didn't seem possible that once he had pitched hay and hauled firewood with Dad through the deep drifts of winter in the bush country.

Then, after more bursts of laughter and words that were just words to me, Jim paused. The smile left his face; and I think everybody suddenly realized that the next part of Jim's speech was going to be different.

"Ladies and gentlemen," Jim said, "when we—your sons and daughters—receive our diplomas tonight, we are supposed to be worthy of them." You could have heard the silence then, thick and fixed and pregnant. "It means," said Jim, "that into our hands you have passed a great trust. When people come to our doctors, they will come, believing that we have not only the skill and knowledge—but the sacred regard for their bodies, to make them well. When you pass your children to our teachers, you will be conferring on us a tremendous—almost a terrible trust." Jim touched a strand of his hair that had fallen across his face. "I once heard a Divinity student say that the greatest prayer was: 'Lord, that I may be worthy.' Now, I know I at last understand."

Somewhere in the student gallery, somebody snickered. But for the rest of that hall, it was as if even breathing had stopped.

"So," Jim went on, "if we are to be worthy, it must mean that we set forth now with a realization of what others have done for us. There should be no room left for false pride. There should be only gratitude for the sacrifices, hidden and open, of all those who had made our education possible . . . who have given us, as it were, to the service of humanity."

Said Jim: "From the bottom of my heart, I want to say to all tonight that whatever I am, I owe to others. To my professors, who have preserved and handed into my keeping the best knowledge of all the generations. To my classmates, who have shown me and shared with me a beautiful friendship. But most of all . . ."

And here Jim paused.

". . . most of all," he said "I want to thank my mother, who is down there in the audience with you. With her permission, ladies and gentlemen—and yours—I'd like to tell you what she has given over the years, for my sake and, I hope, for mankind."

All of a sudden, listening to Jim's voice, I couldn't see. For Jim was up there, not pretending any longer, telling those people who knew the value of education what it meant to be so poor in worldly goods that she'd never owned a washing machine or a toaster or one really lovely dress. She was so unlettered herself she was afraid to speak before strangers. . . . He went on and on, telling them about the lambs and the mosquitoes, till everywhere I looked, I could see women daubing at their eyes and men staring straight ahead so that you knew what it was like with them, too.

When Jim was done, the silence followed him off the stage. Then the applause began. It swept in waves through the auditorium, till at last the distinguished-looking man stepped back and lifted his hands for silence.

"This," he said, "is an occasion of which memories are made—a graduation I shall always remember with pride. May I just say how sincerely honoured we are to have the mothers of our students with us. They, it seems, are behind the 'somebodies' of the world." For a moment, the distinguished-looking man seemed caught up in memories of his own. Then he smiled. "Perhaps it is a good thing for all our graduates to remember," he concluded, "that the riches of education are not meant for the educated alone. They should be given generously to all—but especially to all the unknowns who made our education possible."

Mother was lost completely in admiration of him. In him, she saw a reflection of what Jim would be some day.

At that, I guess it turned out to be the most wonderful trip she'd ever had. On the train going home, she wanted to sit and remember. For her, the years of sacrifice were forgotten; perhaps they had never been. I suppose she thought the only reason Jim's friends and associates had sought her out was because they were so proud of Jim. And when Jim brought up the distinguished-looking man and introduced him as the Dean of his faculty, Mother actually loosened up under his spell. The Dean bowed when he left her, and for years afterwards Mother referred to him with pride, as "a lovely man." It was the one subject she could comment on with a certain assurance, especially when Dad would begin talking to people of the constructive correspondence he used to carry on with some of the best professors in Alberta, in his earlier years on the farm.

Yes, for Mother it was a wonderful train ride home. For me, I thought it would never end. Mother was still in such a daze the day after the graduation that I stuffed myself on banana splits, ice cream, green apples and candy. I could hardly remember to tell Dad that Jim was counting on coming back to the farm for at least a couple of months before he decided what to do with his education, now that he'd got it. Dad said it was good value for a dollar, all the way.

Her Last
Visit Home

The sons and daughters of the pioneer homesteaders began to grow up and go away. . . some even to try their luck in Hollywood. At a time when a signal change in farming ways was making itself evident in the west—the old threshing machines were giving way to combines even in the bush country, where the grain ripened unevenly—I wanted to catch both the end of an era and the changing life styles. I sent this short story first to the Star Weekly *where I was sure Gwen Cowley, the fiction editor, would not be able to resist it. It came back some six weeks later—and I ultimately found out why. (Those editors had not been sent a short story of mine before—and as one of them said: "This is too good to be a first fiction!") Not knowing this, and feeling I had misjudged its appeal, I sent it to* Extension *in the U.S., listed as one of America's 100 best markets. It was bought at an excellent price — and no sooner was it in print in* Extension *than the* Star Weekly *sent a wire, asking if they could reprint it! It is chosen not because of this unique twist in author-editor relations but because I believe this story does capture that changing era, when the threshing machine and a way of life were going out together.*

I'll walk from here," she told the taxi driver at the tarred wooden bridge over the creek, dry now and piled with old leaves. "I'll send for my bags later."

The driver nodded, then recognition started in his eyes. "Aren't you the Monahan girl? The one who went East and became a singer?" His voice was wondering. "To think I used to drive you kids to school!"

Mary Ellen paid him and thought, *Ten years is a long time.* She watched the ancient taxi disappear slowly down the hard road. There was an ember sky behind the burnished poplar clumps on the banks of the creek. North of the trees was the wheat field; and just up on the hill, on the left, was the old farmstead where she had been born.

On the opposite side of the bridge was Martin Hall's farm, but you couldn't see the buildings from the hollow. She wondered if Martin were married yet. . . .

It was September and time for the harvest frosts at night. Mary Ellen could hear the screech of Hungarian partridges as they darted along the bull-wheel tracks in the wheat stubble.

She had intended, really, to come back often. But the years fly! Especially when you are young, with the world at your feet. When people envy you as one of the most popular nightclub singers in New York. When you appear in Hollywood shorts, with promise of a starring role soon. Men to take you wherever you want to go and make you forget the first thrill of a kiss near a line-fence where the raspberries hung thick and ripe.

Maybe that was the real reason she'd forgotten to come back. Because Martin had sent her away. "You've got your chance at the stars—take it," he'd said. "If you don't, you'll always be sorry."

It had seemed impossible sometimes that she could get over the farm so quickly and the people she knew. Her letters home became hurried notes, and those farther apart. And there had been other romances, sophisticated, but short-lived always. She was glad now she hadn't said yes.

A walk in the rain, a cold impatiently neglected—infection—and they told her she would never sing again. Well, she had taken all a career could offer; she had paid the price, and there would be no regrets.

She was up on the hill by the sagging old gate now. Poor Daddy! Despite all his efforts, despite all the money she had sent him, even his fences were still run down. After a lifetime of effort, he hadn't made much from the farm. A hard living, at best.

Well, no regrets, but some things to be sorry for. She'd given so little to them, really. At first, after the music world acclaimed her voice, she'd been glad to send her father the money he needed for some cherished project.

He was always going to buy a new silo, or dreaming of another quarter of land. He wanted to add to the barn, or he had seen some lovely purebred cattle. . . . None of his dreams ever materialized, of course. Even Mary Ellen, throwing her money away, remembered how easily dollars slipped through her father's fingers. And there were always the usual setbacks on the farm, and the crop years just had never been good, it seemed.

Her mother's letters, after awhile, were those of a friend to a city acquaintance. With the exhausting grind of night life to tear great voids out of her time, Mary Ellen had never been able to detach herself to write the letters that would help to heal the breach.

Sometimes, when her father wrote and asked for still another donation, she'd feel the cool hand of loneliness squeeze about her heart. She had understood her mother feeling the unnamed fears only women know. Mary Ellen had gone into a world where other things were more important and where she might easily be embarrassed by her farm folks. But her father always managed to keep the banter and affection in his letters. Was it, Mary Ellen wondered, partly because he needed her financial help?

Not that she cared about the money. But she had prayed then, desperately: *Dear God, let him still love me for the little girl I was, and because I'm his daughter now.*

Sometimes, in those earlier moments, she had seemed on the verge of realizing what true values really were. Then the phone would ring— someone was throwing another party, and Mary Ellen just had to sing.

After the first year only once did she hear from Martin. Her mother was ill, had hurt her back—could she come at once?

And she had wired back—it shamed her to remember now—that she just couldn't, right then. They were opening a new show that might lead to a Hollywood contract. She sent a check big enough to pay for all the help Mom needed and for a regular nurse besides.

Martin had sent his last note then. "I think she would have appreciated *you* more. Money can't buy love, Mary Ellen."

She remembered she had been very angry. She had wept a little and torn Martin's note. "I'll show you," she said. He had told her to follow her destiny, hadn't he?

Well, time and fate had shown her. Overnight her world was gone. The movie studios scrapped the short they were making, and she was very much alone. When the specialists were paid, she'd had just enough for train fare home.

Incredible when you thought of it. She'd wasted her talent, her youth, her money. And she had no right to go back to the farm, to fall back on their sympathy and charity. She had cut herself off from their world and didn't belong.

But for one visit. . . . And then, go. Go quickly, and never return. . . .

There was a man walking slowly from the barn to the house, carrying two pails of milk. He was an old man, with a pipe clenched tightly in his teeth, as if the pails were getting too heavy for him.

"Daddy!" As she had when she was a little girl, Mary Ellen ran to throw herself in his arms. He stopped and set the milk down slowly; and then he smiled as if she had just come home from school.

"Welcome home, Mary Ellen." His voice trembled a little. "Mother, it's Mary Ellen—home!"

From the shadows of the kitchen porch, her mother emerged like a frail little ghost. She kissed Mary Ellen and took in her smart, expensive clothes, and smiled and said, "How are you, Mary Ellen?" like a stranger being kind and extra neighbourly.

"I didn't write," Mary Ellen explained cheerfully. "I wanted to surprise you."

Her father shifted the pipe in his mouth in a luxury of movement, and her mother nodded, but it was plain to see her mind was on the state of the house. "If I'd known, I'd have it tidied up." Like one neighbour woman apologizing to another. "We've been so busy getting ready for the threshers."

Mary Ellen didn't tell them she couldn't sing any more, that she was through. She told them she'd needed a taste of the country air again and asked if she could help separate the milk. Her father said, "No, darling, you'll get your clothes splashed." But gently.

She thought her mother might have the supper dishes in the sink, but they were all done. "There's some pies in the oven for the threshers, though," she smiled at Mary Ellen. "Could you keep an eye on them?"

That was the sort of thing you asked a neighbour to do, out of politeness.

After the outside chores were done, and the pies cooling, and the separator washed, they went into the living room, as if Mary Ellen were special company. She knew her father was weary and needed his sleep. And her mother's mind was on the threshers coming tomorrow. But this was a ritual they always went through for company.

Above the round table where she'd done her homework as a child, the gas lamp hissed against the ceiling. On the table was the Spanish lace tablecloth she'd sent them when she'd gone on a cruise. Mary Ellen understood why her mother had slipped upstairs to rummage; and she hated the rich oriental rug on the living room floor, and the prints she had sent home, on the wall.

She tried to tell them about the city and the show business world and how much she had tried to get back to see them before. Her mother expressed polite awe, but there was pride in her father's eyes—and she realized suddenly that was all she had ever given them or her community: something to be proud of. Now, if they only knew it, even that was done.

They told her bits about the neighbours, and she could hardly place the names. Some of the oldtimers had died. Girls she had gone to school with had babies. There was a movie in the town every week now. Saturday would be the big harvest dance.

Only one fact stood out. Martin was unmarried still. Martin had paid for his farm and was doing well. His outfit would thresh for them tomorrow.

Then she realized they were staring at her, realizing she wasn't listening. She flushed awkwardly, but the strangeness was about them even more.

After coffee, which was bitter in her mouth because her mother brought out the fancy chinaware, she went up to her little room under the eaves. Downstairs, she could hear her folks turn in quickly.

She undressed by moonlight and felt the sweet, cool farm air as she struggled into pajamas. The garden lay below her, husked and stripped in the moonlight.

Were they glad to have her back she wondered? Or did they feel the same as when some city friends came out at harvest once and just got in the way? The emptiness inside her was too much for tears.

She had been away too long. Coming home was more than just a matter of buying a railway ticket.

A tractor tackling the upward grade from the bridge and creaking bundle wagons in the yard awakened her. It was nearly 11 a.m. From the window she watched the threshing crew pull through the yard toward the wheat fields. Her father was hurrying to pull a granary out of the yard ahead of them. He had to run to keep up with the straining horses. He stumbled and fell—and Mary Ellen's hand pressed tight against her heart.

Her father was getting slower. But he was gallant, too—he didn't want the younger men to know he was hurt. He was on his feet in a minute.

The young man on the tractor stopped and shouted. He got off, pushing his cap back on his head. He went up and spoke to her father, smiling, and took the lines; and the granary moved away steadily toward the old dry slough in the field where the wheat straw was always blown.

Mary Ellen's heart beat in rhythm to the soft idling of the tractor. Even if she hadn't known, she would have recognized that dark-haired man who still squinted against the September haze.

The smell of food came from downstairs. Mary Ellen hoped that her mother would need her to help with the extra burden of cooking; but Mrs. Evans, a neighbour, was there, domineering the kitchen, hurrying the dinner.

Up in the field, Martin levelled the separator and the first racks were loaded; and then the threshers came toward the house for an early dinner. Mary Ellen slipped on a jacket and went down to the dry creek bed. She couldn't bear the men staring at her through the meal. Most of them were boys she'd gone to school with, but they'd eat with more laughter and ease if she weren't there.

She wandered far up the creek, feeling a kinship with the lost leaves of autumn. By mid-afternoon when she was coming back she saw her mother headed for the field with the men's lunch.

"Mother, I'll take it," she pleaded. She didn't care about the men now. All she wanted to do was to help a little, ease a bit of the stoop from their shoulders. "Oh, Mother, please—"

As her mother paused, it seemed for a moment as if the years had gone and the old comradeship was there between them. She handed the lunch over.

Martin was veering the blower of the quivering separator when she rounded the fresh-blown strawpile. There was dust in Mary Ellen's eyes, and her ankles stung from the stubble.

"How's it going?" Mary Ellen yelled the old greeting.

Martin turned his head slowly and jumped lightly to the ground. His smile was white, in a sweat-streaked face.

"I heard you were back," he said. He yelled at a teamster pulling away from the feeder. "Bill! Java!"

One by one the men ate. Martin climbed the racks and tossed in bundles, while the pitchers had lunch, washing the sandwiches down with great mouthfuls of coffee.

When they were finished, Martin came over beside her. He seemed sure of himself, content. Once she had thought he needed her. She smiled at him now. "Is it threshing well?"

Martin's eyes took interest in her. He shook his head regretfully. "Too dry a year. It'll hardly pay for the threshing."

She saw her dad then, climbing backwards out of the granary. He had been shovelling the wheat away from the grain spout.

She took the coffee over to him, wanting to cry because the men had eaten all the sandwiches. He sat down heavily on the log runner of the granary and drank slowly. There was blood dried on the back of his hand where he'd fallen that morning.

"Daddy, I'm sorry it's not a very good crop." What pitiful, inadequate words to say. If she could just tell him, "Don't worry about it, Daddy. I'll write you out a cheque. . . ."

Her father smiled up at her, patted her hand. "Maybe next year, darling."

It took the threshers a bit over a day to clean up the fields. The sun-kissed, crackling stubble was bare, save for three small strawpiles blown into the sloughs and an odd bundle that had fallen off a jolting rack. Her father walked slowly across the yard.

When Martin had the thresher on the road, he stopped the tractor and climbed lightly over the garden fence, to where she was raking the old potato vines. The silence was vast now, but the hum of the thresher was still in her ears.

"Staying long, Mary Ellen?" His voice was almost impersonal.

She wore old slacks and a kerchief tied loosely round her head, and she leaned on the rake and smiled at him. "I'm not sure, really."

"Long enough for the harvest dance?"

The wind was a breath of long ago. She wondered suddenly if she still loved Martin as she loved the farm and her folks—or if she was only trying to recapture some of the old happiness because she would never sing again. She was confused inside.

"I don't know," she told him.

There was something like pity in his eyes. "No, I guess you wouldn't, Mary Ellen. You'd have such a dull time—with people like us."

He went away then on his tractor, with the separator lunging unsteadily behind. Mary Ellen struck a match to the dried potato stalks and stared into the flames. Somewhere, on the hard dirt roads, grain wagons rattled into town.

After supper that night, she came upon her folks figuring costs for the year. Their talk stopped, and she walked away.

When she heard her father go out to the barn, Mary Ellen slipped back to the kitchen. Her mother was still sitting at the table, staring dully. "It isn't much," she kept saying, "when you've worked so hard."

There was silence in the kitchen for a minute, long and tight. Then her mother pushed her chair away and looked at her, the polite way you always did to your guests, and asked her how long she was staying.

The one opportunity Mary Ellen had hoped for was gone, as far away as the lights of New York, the champagne of Radio City.

Mary Ellen knew they were wondering when she'd leave, so that the comradely routine of their lives could go on again. With her gone, they could show their poverty and share their fears. They could dream of next year, when they might thresh a little more.

She had known it in Martin's voice, too. *"How long are you staying, Mary Ellen?"* Not—"I hope you'll stay a good while with us." When you're gone away, whatever effect you have on the life of this little community will be gone, too. Whatever old dreams and memories you stirred will die again.

She answered carefully, "I'd like to stay till after the harvest dance, Mother." And to herself she added: "And then I'll never bother you again."

That left only a couple of days. And she gave up trying. She could sleep till noon, while her father plowed the stubble under in long brown waves and her mother worked in the root cellar and cleaned the chicken houses. And there was the creek to explore. And one day she climbed the brown hill above it, and there were Martin's buildings, snug and painted and lonely. But oh, how that little farmhouse cried out for curtains on the windows and woodsmoke in the chimney.

The harvest dance was an occasion, and everyone went.

On the Monahan farm, the chores were done early, and nobody said anything when Mary Ellen helped. They dressed in silence, and Mary Ellen drove in the buggy with her mother and dad. She had hoped in her woman's heart that Martin might drive over for her, and then shamefully told herself that Martin's life had gone on just as much as hers—only more completely, and to a better end.

When they got to the hall, Pete Mature's old-time music was gay, and everyone was dancing—the old people and the farm boys and girls and the kids in their strange best suits and dresses. Pete had played the fiddle there since the community was young.

On the crowded floor, her parents excused themselves and danced their first dance together. Mary Ellen watched them happy and brave. A couple of laughing men jostled her, then saw she was a stranger. They apologized. When they jostled other girls, they stopped to tease. The men who weren't dancing stayed near the back of the hall, the girls sat around the sides. She went over and joined them self-consciously. They made way for her politely.

One by one, the boys came up and took the girls away from around her. She was very much alone, and she wondered what had made her come to this dance without an escort. Out here especially, people noticed that.

In the confusion as the first dance ended and the couples found their seats, she was suddenly aware of Martin beside her. In his dark suit, he would have fitted into the nightlife of New York, she thought; and was glad for his sake that he wasn't there.

He held out his hand. "After all, you taught me to dance," he smiled.

So he remembered! She got up gladly, her skirt swirling behind her, and she felt young again and glad inside.

If she hadn't know it before, when Martin's arms were about her, she knew for sure then. A woman could get lost in those arms and never want to find her way back again. No wonder it had been one man after another in New York.

"They're not really bad, these people," Martin's lips murmured in her ear. "Do you know that?"

Mary Ellen said nothing. He thought she was taking in the dance just to break the monotony till she was back in the city again. He thought she only condescended to belong, when with all her heart she wished she could belong again forever.

They were dancing near the platform when the music crashed silent. The dancers turned their faces up to the orchestra. Old Pete Mature, his fiddle in one hand, was at the microphone.

"Folks, I guess we're all right proud to have back for a visit that famous little singing star—the girl who grew up on a neighbourhood farm and went to school with our kids—Mary Ellen Monahan!"

They gave her a good hand, the way they always did for visitors to their town; but slow terror froze Mary Ellen's heart.

"We'd like Mary Ellen to come up here and sing a number for us." Pete beckoned to her. "Remember, folks, she was singing here the night someone discovered her and took her away."

The crowd remembered that with warm recollection. They relaxed a little, buzzed, laughed lightly.

"Go on, Mary Ellen." Martin's voice urged her, the way he had that first night, long ago. She'd been scared then, but not as frightened as now. "They're waiting."

Mary Ellen turned urgently to him, striving for poise. "I can't Martin!" It was so necessary he understand. "Martin, tell them something—tell them anything—"

"Surely you could sing one song for these people who gave you a start!" he whispered.

Something snapped in her then. She didn't care any more. After tonight it would never matter again.

She walked up on the platform, through the orchestra, smiling very brightly. She brushed Pete's hand lightly aside and spoke into the microphone. "I'd give any contract I ever signed just to sing once more for you." She could feel the excitement among them now. "You gave me my start, and I forgot you. I didn't mean to, but I did. . . ." She said all the things she would remember with shame afterwards. The hall was deathly still, the way it is when people are too embarrassed to move.

And when she was finished, Pete started the music quickly. But not before something came loose in the people. They started clapping suddenly—then steadily, again and again.

And now it sounded—it sounded as if they were clapping *for* her, telling her they understood. It was just as if they realized a neighbour was in trouble—

She had to get away then, before the smiling mask she'd worn had slipped. Mercifully, there was the side door, and the maples behind the hall, and the cool wind on her cheeks. After a minute her breathing was fairly even.

"Baby!" It was her dad coming through the night toward her. His old arms enfolded her. He was talking to her softly, saying sweet wonderful things. About how he had guessed everything wasn't well. Particularly when she never offered any money this time. "That was your apology in the past," he told her gently.

And then he was saying that long ago he figured young people couldn't keep on at the pace she was going without burning out. But childeren were hard to advise. So all the money he'd got from her—why, he didn't take it for silos and farms; he'd put it in a trust fund for the time when she would need it.

"Oh, Daddy!" Tears of joy were scalding in her throat. And then suddenly the music behind her was good, and the night full of promise. She laughed shakily.

"Oh, Daddy, please let me make it up to you and Mother. Oh, please!"

Her mother was there then, too. It looked as if she had been crying a mite; and it had been a long, long time since Mary Ellen had seen her mother cry. "Mary Ellen, does it mean that you're home to stay? That you'll not be leaving us again soon?"

"Now, Mother!" her father admonished. "Mary Ellen's young yet." And his voice was young, too. "But maybe she won't go too far away—maybe just across the road." He nudged Mary Ellen. "See that farmer boy headed this way? I think he's looking for you, Baby—and if ever I saw love in a man's eyes, I saw it when you were up on that stage, facing the toughest crowd in the world—the folks at home."

They left her there by the windy maples, under the extravagant autumn sky. And when Martin reached out to touch her, a new song started in Mary Ellen's heart—the song of a woman loved and wanted and home to stay.

◆◆◆◆

You Never
Walk Alone

The only thing I ever saw really dividing the bushwhackers were politics, where, without realizing the fact, they were dividing only over methods. Additionally, I felt compassion for the few women who tried their hand at getting elected, generally with discouraging results. I felt by now that I should be trying to depict all facets of life among the people who opened up the west—and this story was the result. Authors are never too sure of markets at the best of times, so I never even sent it to Toronto. Instead it was sent to a wonderful fiction editor, Amy J. Roe, of The Country Guide, *who promptly bought it. "I hope," she wrote, "you can read this letter through my fresh tears."*

They were coming close to the legislative building now: down 109th Street, crowded with traffic: past the modernistic new Administration Building . . . in sight of the dome. Traffic funnelled toward the High Level Bridge and, when it broke for a moment, the flower-bedecked grounds and the olive-coloured stone of the province's seat of government were before her. Suddenly, panic was welling up in her—panic such as she'd never known before.

Old Andy Carter, her father, was none too sure about city driving, and he pulled over to the flower beds, looking for a place to park. There were cars everywhere. Over near a side entrance, she saw a tall, thin man step out of a long black car; the premier . . . and near the front steps, a group of laughing, well-dressed men whose faces looked somehow familiar: old campaigners, who would sit around her, and in front of her, in the legislative chambers. Those were the faces who had thundered at her on public platforms, who had ridiculed and laughed.

The panic came back. It caught at her throat, then choked through her body: and she wanted to run.

"Kay." Her father's voice steadied her. "When you walk up those steps today, you're no ordinary visitor any more." There was pride in his voice, but awe, too. "Of all the dreams I ever dared to have, not one included any of my kids becoming a representative of the people!"

Danny, wedged between his mother and Mary-Lee on the back seat, whistled.

"Yeah, imagine! A lady politician—wow, ain't that something!"

She turned, suddenly loving him as she had never loved her ten-year-old brother before. She smiled shakily.

"Danny, I'm scared enough. Don't you let me down, too." On this day she shouldn't be talking like that, but she had to unburden her fears to someone. "The opposition aren't going to be easy on me because of my sex. There are smart newspapermen in the Liberals— and the Conservatives are nearly all lawyers—and—even in the elections, the Social Crediters called me a neurotic old maid!"

"You should care!" Fourteen-year-old Mary-Lee, to whom the depression was unbelievable, tossed her head with teen-age contempt. "We'll be up in the gallery busting our buttons off . . ."

"Maybe that's what I'm scared of," Kay said. "Except for you, I—I feel so alone. I mean, you naturally think I'm wonderful, but what do I know, really? Somehow people voted for me . . ."

"And do you think the people were wrong, Kay?"

Her father patted her hand. He couldn't know how she worried about them—those people who had put their faith in her. If she failed them—if she went back and saw in their eyes, not devotion but disillusionment. . . .

Trying to ease the tension, she glanced at her watch. Still plenty of time before the pomp and ceremony of the Opening. She wondered if she should go up to the Members' cloakrooms—if somebody would tell her what to do—how to enter. If they didn't . . . she bit her lip. Well, she could watch the others. She'd take her seat. She'd see the sergeant-at-arms carrying in the mace: symbol of a sovereign people's power.

"God of all good!" The prayer burst uncontrollably inside her. *"Never let me forget what I'm doing here. Every time I get up to speak, put truth on my tongue . . ."* She daubed at the tears in her eyes. *I musn't cry now. Let me at least walk in there as if I was deserving*

of the part.

"Kay . . . why don't you walk around for a minute?" her mother said softly. "Takes the tension out of a body. I remember when your father and I were getting married. I just cried and walked for weeks before it . . ."

"And I cried for weeks after it," said her father.

They were trying to help her, and she was grateful. She got out of the car and her feet were irrevocably drawn toward the wide stone steps. She kept back from the crowds, then looked to see if her family were watching.

They were. Danny locked his hands in victory style, and she smiled again. Her mother was giving orders from the back seat. Her father shrugged resignedly, and the car moved forward, disappearing around the driveway overlooking the broad rolling North Saskatchewan River.

She was alone.

People kept crowding past her, neither glancing at her nor recognizing her, and the moment was unreal. She looked up at the dome and thought wonderingly; when did it begin? Not when the election results came in—when the excitement crept even into the broadcaster's voice. "And in the northern constituencies, a dark horse is sweeping the polls—Kathleen Carter, who campaigned on a straight service ticket. . . ." Not even when she first decided to go in for politics. "If you don't win, Kay, we'll have to leave the country!" That was Mary-Lee's send-off.

No, she thought; *it began a long time ago . . . when I was just a little girl and Daddy drove us into Edmonton as a special treat.*

Barry Williams had been with them: and the way the two kids held hands and looked up at the dusty dome, you'd have thought it was a church. Barry was 12—only a year older than Kay—and so serious and stuck-in-the-mud that usually he made her mad.

Barry was from the farm next to Carters'—a poor farm, where he trapped muskrats on the marshy bottoms to buy schoolbooks. He'd never been to Edmonton before—maybe that was why he stood like that, his eyes never leaving the dome.

"Kids," Andy Carter said, "lots of folks pass here every day and never even look over. Me . . . I would like to get down on the ground and say a prayer of thanks to all the men—mostly little men who never knew what the good things of life were—who died, passing on a little bit more freedom to us. They aren't done, kids. The need for them didn't end when they made King John sign the Magna Carta or stood up with pitchforks and longbows and cut down the feudal lords. Kids, their kind have got to go on while men are left . . . or everything they gave us will be taken away.''

It was a strange speech to Kay. Lots of times she wondered if her father talked like that just to find recompense for the loneliness of farming, or if he really believed it deep in his soul. She would have been embarrassed if he had talked like that before a lot of neighbours, and unaccountably she was annoyed because Barry nodded so sagely.

"You don't even know what he's talking about!" she said.

But she couldn't provoke Barry that day. All the way home he was silent, reliving, she guessed, the wonders of what he had seen. And that night, doing chores, she suddenly asked her father why he had taken Barry to Edmonton.

Her father, carrying two milk pails, looked toward the Williams' fence. She followed his gaze . . . and she could see a boy walking slowly behind a line of scrub-cattle—a boy with a stick in his hand and a book before his eyes. Long before her father spoke, she felt inexplicable tears touching her lashes.

"Every night at chore time, I see him like that," Andy Carter said. "I never had much education myself. Maybe that's why."

She stood there, while her father went into the barn and Barry passed out of sight, and a strange new emotion stirred in her heart. Suddenly she wanted to go to him—to drive home the cows so he could read. She wanted to cry. Instead, she went to the house and asked her mother if a girl could fall in love at age 11.

That summer she was a tall and spirited girl—lingering along the road-side till Barry started for school—studying at nights till she put her head in her hands and wept, hoping she would get marks as good as his. Her biggest dream in life revolved around a new dress for the harvest dance with Barry.

Then one evening, when the prairie chickens were sitting on the tumbly new straw piles and coloured leaves were piling high in the dry ditches, she came home from school to find the fire in the wood stove cold and her mother crying.

The crop had been the best ever; they had raised three times as many hogs as the year before. But her dad couldn't meet the taxes, much less the installment on the mortgage. When she finally dared to ask about the dress, her mother told her, gently, that maybe next year. . . .

It was Barry who prophesied that next year would be a long time coming. Somewhere in the unreality of dyeing flour sacks into dresses and looking into lard-pail lunch buckets at the familiar prairie-chicken sandwiches with the darkish meat, Barry had to quit school. He was in Grade Eight that year and at the top of his class, but his dad was poorly and he had to work out the taxes on the road gangs or the municipality would sell the farm. One night she passed him riding home on a wagon and she was hurt because he didn't speak or smile. Then she saw he was asleep. He was too thin and too tired for hard work with the fresnoes, but he never complained.

She thought she would get used to walking down the road with other boys, but she didn't. In the end, she started visiting his mother, in the evenings when he had finished the chores. Always he surrounded himself with pamphlets and books, but she thought he was grateful for someone who listened, who tried to believe what he was saying.

"We produced too much, Kay—too much wheat, too much coal, too much beef . . . too many tools and inventions to keep on producing too much! I think the reason we can't distribute is because our economic system is geared to another age."

Her father—who had voted Liberal, Conservative and UFA as he considered advisable—was talking the new theory of Social Credit, too. The idea of trying something new appealed to him.

"We got life here, Nellie," he'd orate to Kay's mother, as if she was an audience. "We got new bloods, great imagination, resources unlimited. Why not try something, anyway? You keep trying, you never know what you'll stumble onto."

Kay asked Barry if he was a Social Crediter. "I dont' know— yet," Barry said. "It'll stimulate something, anyway."

Out of the confusion of meetings (held in the schoolhouse) and propaganda (delivered with the mail) there was one incident Kay would never forget. It was the night Barry spoke, impassionedly, to still another schoolhouse meeting; and old Letts, the storekeeper, got up, shaking, and said Barry was talking Social Credit because he was a poverty-stricken rabble-rouser looking for something for nothing.

Barry—still not too far from the classroom where ideas were everything—seemed to wilt. For the first time it must have dawned on him that the sincerity of a man's politics would usually be judged by what he had, not by the ideal that motivated him. He passed his hand over his eyes—he turned and went outside.

She found him sitting on the old teeter-totter beside the swings— like a little boy, she thought, left alone by his playmates. She knew he had been crying, and her hate was fierce.

"Let them suffer! Oh, they're stupid . . . ignorant . . . Barry . . ."

After a minute, almost wonderingly, he turned and comforted her. His fingers touched her dark hair, bronzed suddenly by a full spring moon above the schoolhouse.

"Kay! You know . . . you're so beautiful!"

The hate in her was gone—melted—and bliss was pouring through her. She put her arms around his neck, and he caught her fingers to his lips.

"I shouldn't have run away," Barry said thoughtfully. "Kay, nothing worthwhile ever came from running away from a problem . . ."

There were other incidents, too. She saw, with a shock, her father growing grey. Her mother worked without letup, as if determined to beat the depression by herself. Kay herself learned how to make flour sacks into slips and dresses, how to pack a "tick" with straw—so it was almost as comfortable as a real mattress.

One day a thin man in black tacked the first "Sheriff's Lien" she had ever seen on Bob Conway's granary. The next morning Mrs. Conway came running down the road, screaming. Without waiting to hear her story, Kay's father rushed down to Conway's. Bob had shot himself.

She kept waking at nights after that, cold and shivering; and when she couldn't stand it any longer, she went to Barry. They talked a long time, and then he said stubbornly:

"He shouldn't have run away."

It sounded terrible—terrible till he added: "Kay, you were meant to give love and laughter. I want you to remember that love is the answer to death, hope the answer to despair."

She found comfort in his words. She believed him.

There were more meetings in the schoolhouse—and Mrs. Letts wouldn't let her husband go any more: it was bad for the store. Barry spoke again and they listened. One night their sitting member, a UFA man, came. White-haired and worried, he told the farmers how he had served them, how the cabinet had seriously considered the Social Credit proposals and found them impossible to implement, at least in a province. He begged them not to be stampeded.

There was a terrible silence. No questions. No criticisms. They thanked him, then turned to ask Barry to say a few words . . . and no one noticed when the UFA men slipped out the door.

"They're going to nominate that boy!" Andy Carter said to her one day. "By jingo, they are!" She could hardly believe her father.

If Barry got the nomination and won . . . Barry would need—a wife!

The night of the nominating convention, the meeting was moved to the community hall. The town was filled with Bennett buggies and wagons and old cars and men in the corners. In the hall itself, the tension made Kay sick—the closeness, and the voices, and her eyes trying to follow Barry.

It wasn't until the nominations were almost ended that she realized Barry's name hadn't been put forth. She saw him arguing with one man after another, and he didn't look happy. The chairman looked exasperated and tired and angry. Finally he pointed down to the sea of faces, and Barry got up.

"Folks, apparently I have to make it clear publicly that I don't want to be nominated." The shock made a ringing silence in the hall. Barry's face looked haggard. "It's hard to explain why. Maybe because I'm not ready. All I know is it isn't my role. I will support whoever you nominate. . . ."

Taking her home at last, as the wet June damp cooled her tired face, he tried to make her understand.

"Kay, the UFA's going out to the last man and the Social Crediters are coming in."

"Well, then, why—Barry, you know more about Social Credit than any of them!"

He was very tired. "It came to me the night our own UFA man talked to us. Those men were just as good as any we're nominating. Kay, they're fine, sincere men. We're making a mistake somewhere. We're dividing on methods. . . ."

In her silence, he saw her tears. "Kay! Kay!" He caught her to him. "Listen to me. It hasn't anything to do with loving you and wanting you. I'm not walking out on life—or asking you to. We have a right to be married—and we will be, Kay, we will! But don't you see? We owe something to humanity, too. . . . All I ask is that you wait another couple of years. Maybe two, three years at the most. . . ."

She pulled the page off the calendar in the living room—April, 1939. The two years had stretched into four, because Barry's father died, and he couldn't leave the family in a ruin of debts. But it was past now. Her mother was sewing on the dress—the most beautiful dress she had ever seen—her wedding dress of white.

"Just 210 more days!" She was radiant—even inside she felt radiant. "Mom, couldn't we have a June wedding?"

"Your father and I had a June wedding," her mother snipped the thread with her teeth. "Can't say as he was different than July or October husbands." She turned to Kay and the lined face softened. "October will get here, dear. You know June is a bad month for weddings in the bushland—too much seeding to be done. But after the crop's off. . . ."

There was a step on the porch. Barry knocked and came in. He kissed her and grinned, but she was tuned to his every emotion now and she sensed the undercurrent of unhappiness.

"Barry! You couldn't get a meeting lined up!"

"Everybody's too busy to think—or study." For a moment he was that serious little boy looking at the dome, and she was vexed with him. "The big flurry's over. The dividend bills were disallowed and I think the government's relieved. Even old Letts talks to me now!"

He saw the look on her face, the unbelief that had been growing more and more within her of late. "Kay honey . . ."

"Haven't you done enough?" She couldn't keep the accusations back. "Haven't you wasted enough of our lives—on books and your folks and—and politics! For heavens sake, Barry, you haven't got time to be educating people, especially when they don't want to be educated!"

She was sorry then. Patiently Barry explained to her anew what he had come to believe. That the people should elect a good man, get behind him and support him, regardless of his party. Little by little progress would come.

"Think how easy the members would have it, too, Kay. They wouldn't have to worry about election propaganda, just as long as they obeyed. . . ." His eyes fastened on Kay's mother by the sewing machine. "Hey! What's that?"

"Out of here, you!" Mrs. Carter spread herself over the dress. "You're not supposed to see this till October. It's unlucky!"

The war arrived in September, and he went away when the harvest was only half-done. She walked with him to the station; and passing the church, Barry stopped suddenly and held her tight, as if out of all the unreality of their lives, he had wakened to what he was losing.

"Kay, we should have been married there! Just because a leader went mad. . . ."

She didn't want to talk any more about politics and leaders and men. His lips touched her hair, and she thought, *It's really true. He's going away—and he's taking with him that smile and those strong arms.* . . .

"Don't you see—just so our daughters won't have to go through it all again? Kay, do you believe me—I've learned how to wait. There won't be anyone else, no matter how lonely or how scared I get over there. . . ."

She lived for the train whistle that brought the blue V-mail from Barry. Sometimes with his love he sent another book that made long references to how men united for war and fought one another for peace.

"To serve—to serve!" Sometimes the writing seemed to turn into his impassioned words. "Kay, that is the secret: we must learn to serve one another. . . ."

She was going for the cows one day when, suddenly, she began to understand what he was talking about. If men could give as much to the old and the helpless, to the hungry and the naked, as they gave in death and destruction on the battlefields of war. . . .

If they made the sacrifices, short of life itself, for medicine, for education, for their country. . . . If you stopped worrying about yourself and made your neighbour your worry. . . .

"That's it!" The jubilance jumped from Barry's answer to her letter. "Maybe it'll take 'em a long time to really understand, Kay. It's hard to get rid of prejudice and distrust—the feeling you're being a sucker—that nobody else cares. The Galilean told them a long time ago: 'Bear ye one another's burdens. . . . ' "

That was the week young Len Conway came out from Edmonton to visit his old neighbours. He and his mother had a nice home in the west end. Len boasted that the house was worth double what they paid for it. He was making good money working in an aircraft-repair plant and he was a union organizer—which didn't interest her till he began to talk about the war's end and the strikes that would come.

"Strikes," Len said, "that will clean out all the dirty rotten inequality at last."

"Will they do any good?" Kay was amazed at the sharpness in her voice. "Len, your bosses must have problems, too—shortages and red tape and inefficiency and high taxes. Lots of businesses go bankrupt every year. They're the people who feed you. . . ."

Len Conway's look was terrible. "You sound like an anti-labour spokesman!"

"Len! When did I ever know anything but labour? And hard-times—and heartbreak?" She was getting emotional, but she couldn't help it. "I should be looking after a husband and children now—not just—just withering up inside. . . ."

Even the clumsy sympathy in his eyes couldn't hide the resolution. "I know. That's what I'm trying to tell you. As long as I live, I'll never forget they're the ones who killed my father."

The trembling it set up inside her didn't go away till Barry's letters came again.

Something strange had been happening to her. Barry was gone, but he had the power to bring himself beside her always. She did not care because she seldom went to dances now. Barry was more alive to her than the new crop of youths.

She read the books he told her to read: saw, at last, the dream he wanted her to see. It was a vision of proud people—the Canadian people that Barry loved—propserous and free and strong . . . strong by their own power.

"Don't be afraid to dream, my darling. And dream big, dear one. Only dreams come true—everything else passes away. Tell farmer to stop fighting farmer. Tell labour to stop fighting management. Tell them to work together, for cach other and, so, for themselves. . . ."

Sunset was streaking the bushland when the telegram came. The air was sweet and calm. In those words, blurring before her eyes, she could hear his voice again, over all the years, kind and patient, humble and strong, talking of that dream that was not given to many to see.

"Sometimes they come from among our own, Kay." It was her father behind her—her father staring toward the old line-fence. "Maybe studying in a little log cabin in Illinois. Maybe walking across the barren bushland with a book before their eyes. . . ."

Sunlight was striking the dull dome of the legislative building. She looked around in a blur of tears, to find her family had come up behind her. They had known she needed this moment, these memories, to herself.

"Ready now?" her mother asked.

People were converging on the steps, men and women of many political beliefs, all down for the historic and gala opening.

"Barry would have been proud of you." Her mother's lips were trembling. "So many voted for you, dear."

She smiled reassuringly at them, straightened her shoulders. She turned to the entrance and suddenly the people before her were all the people who had voted for her . . . not because of what she promised, but because she had made them believe in themselves.

She would make mistakes and she would be clumsy . . . she would get tired and disheartened—but they would speak through her, and they would be her strength. Alone? Not now—not ever.

Because of them—and a dream—she would never walk alone.

A Man
Is Born

The bushwhacker's sons and daughters had fears and struggles of their own, when they left the bushland for what was, in many ways, the much more difficult world of the big city. This, in the midst of the baby boom, was meant to portray the maturing of one of them.

Joe Delaney, father of five—at least the fifth had been impending when he fell groggily across the bed at 3:30 a.m.—came slowly out of the stupor of sleep and worry to find black bangs and brown eyes hovering by his bedside.

"Daddy, gimme my penny. I'm dry!"

Joe raised himself stupidly.

"Feel, Daddy! Am I not wet?" A new tone crept into Bridget's 3-year-old voice. "Where's Mommy?"

"Mommy? I'll tell you a secret about Mommy, at breakfast. . . ."

"She's gone for our baby," Bridget said positively.

"Yeah," said Joe. "So let's you and I get breakfast, real quiet."

It was too late. From the room Bridget had just left came a churring sound, much like a happy squirrel in a far-away spruce. Toosers—originally christened Theresa—wasn't going to miss out on any morning loving.

Joe staggered past the dresser, glancing at his gaunt, unshaven reflection. Ann was inside every bit of his being again: Ann, heavy and tired, and telling him not to worry, to go home and sleep.

"Aroo . . . ooh!" The crib bars began to rattle. "Roo . . ."

"Coming, Toosers, coming!"

From the door of the girls' room, Joe surveyed her fat littleness, the cherubic smile, the mist of golden hair. With an art any Hollywood starlet would have envied, Toosers slowly closed her right eye in a beguiling wink.

"Dear Lord, what wonderful kids!" Joe went over and lifted her. "To think there's another one coming to join you."

He sent up a little prayer for Ann, trying not to think of why Doc Elkhorn hadn't phoned; paid Bridget her penny, started dressing Toosers, and pushed the porridge pot on the stove. He felt scared, almost sick inside. It never got any better when Ann went to the hospital. It always got worse.

He was just getting the salt into the porridge when a sibilant hissing sounded from the boys' room upstairs. The "Sss-ss-sss!" was shattered by a growl that 14 months earlier (when Toosers was being born) had caused the helper from the *Ready-Made Mothers Bureau* to drop the dishes and quit.

"Miles!" The growl emanated from far inside seven-year-old Mark who, in the morning, couldn't stand any noise, least of all what four-year-old Miles called "whistling."

"Boys!" Joe raced to the foot of the stairway. "Mark, you get dressed for school, up there. Miles, bring your clothes down here."

"Dunno where dey are." By the tone of his voice, Miles couldn't have cared less.

"There, you stupid!" Upstairs, Mark went ferociously to his father's aid.

The whistling started again, followed by another growl and a rush of bare feet across the floor, a yelp from Miles, another command from Joe, then the thud of Miles descending. Despite his years, he weighed two pounds more than Mark, and not much of it was fat.

He gave Joe a sunny smile. "Hi, Dad!"

"Hi," Joe said. There were times he envied Miles his carefree nature, but this wasn't one of them. "Where's the rest of your clothes?"

Miles looked down with a certain wonderment at one curled-up shoe, one yellow sock and a tattered pair of jeans (inside out).

"Upstairs," said Miles. "I guess." He stuck his head into his parents' bedroom. "Hi, Mommy." Quick as a flash, the blue eyes swung to Joe. "Daddy, where's Mommy?"

"It's a secret," said Joe, picking up the porridge spoon. "I'll tell you all at breakfast."

The baby should have been born by now. Why haven't they phoned? She said she wasn't scared, but she was, this time. And worried about the kids, about the bills, about me. Ann . . . Ann!

It took him a full half hour to get them arranged at the table in the tiny breakfast nook. Miles, on his thrice-reglued stool, in the far corner; then Bridget; Toosers at the end, in her blue plastic bib and highchair; then, on this side, his place and Mark's. Lots of room for Mark and him this morning, but where would they ever crowd one more stool or highchair into this kitchen?

Mark, his brows still ominous, was the last to the table. He was dressed, except for his shoes. (One morning he had started off for school without them.) He carried a colouring book under his arm.

Miles hailed him like a long-lost friend. "Mornin', Marky!"

"Shut up! Morning, Dad."

"Good morning," Joe said. He looked at his oldest son suspiciously. "Were you colouring in bed?"

"He was weadin'," said Miles.

"Shut up! I was not reading. I was studying my spelling."

After 9 months at school, Mark could add, subtract and spell like a fourth-grader. If you didn't stop him, he took his books to the table, into the bathroom, even to bed. For a moment time turned back for Joe.

You once had that ability to concentrate, remember? Before you met Ann . . . before these kids . . . and that jerk's job with the J.P. Adams Advertising Agency. . . .

He came out of his thoughts to hear Miles and Bridget tell Mark that Momma had gone for their new baby. Mark turned to his father, his voice rising like a bird's. "Has she, Daddy?"

Joe assured him it was so. Bridget's brown eyes crinkled tenderly. "What would you like? A baby brother, or a baby sister?"

Bridget was too enchanted to care: Momma had promised she could bathe the baby. Miles pushed his porridge bowl well into the center of the table, knocked his head experimentally on the table top, stuck an elbow ecstatically into Bridget's stomach.

"I want a wittle baby brother!"

Bridget screamed. "Get your 'bow out of my stomach!"

Miles gave her an incredulous look. "My 'bow? What's zat?"

Joe stopped the indignant yells of Bridget, the "shut ups" of Mark. "She means your elbow," he explained to Miles. "Don't you, honey?"

The brown eyes lit up for Joe . . . they always lit up for their daddy.

"Daddy, what did I not used to say for baloney?"

"'Taboney," said Joe. "Now eat your—"

"And what did I not used to say for snowsuit?"

"Snowsnoot," obliged Joe. "Kids, eat your—"

The telephone shrilled. Joe knocked over his chair, racing for it.

It was Radio Survey calling, wanting to know what station he was listening to. Joe hung up slowly, his heart thumping against his ribs.

He got back to the kitchen, just as the last of the porridge in Toosers' bowl was dripping reluctantly to the floor. Toosers smiled with the most beguiling wink Joe had ever seen on any woman, young or old. But he couldn't smile back.

How did Ann stand it? How would she make out with still another?

He had got Mark off to school, the others dressed and outside, and the dishes in the sink, when the phone rang again. It was his boss at the Adams Advertising Agency.

The morning growl in J.P.'s voice was increasingly capable of starting something eating deep down in Joe's stomach. He explained to J.P. that Shirley, Ann's sister, would get in from the farm tomorrow and that, meanwhile, he had to watch the kids.

"Phone some agency." The voice was curt. "You're supposed to start the Babson account today."

"Agencies charge too much," Joe said, with more stiffness than he'd used for a long time. "Besides, they don't understand the kids. The little ones especially aren't used to them. If I'm here—"

"If your salary is that inadequate," J.P. said ominously, "I'm at a loss to understand how you can afford still another child. I might add, Mr. Delaney, I can hire any number of qualified people for a lot less than I'm paying you now."

When Joe hung up the phone finally, he was shaking, and so scared his palms were damp. What did it matter to Adams that some strange woman, no matter how capable, couldn't be expected to understand that when Toosers raised her hands dramatically to heaven, it was time to rush her to the bathroom? To Adams, there would be nothing deeply moving about Bridget's back-to-front elfin talk. Adams had no children of his own. And that crack about affording another baby. . . .

The helplessness of his position hit him anew. Where had all the confidence of his college years gone? Every month the bills were getting bigger and farther behind. The house was too small. He thought of Babson of Ali Baba Homes, whose new advertsing campaign he should have started today.

More than 12 months ago, Babson had driven out to see Joe about a display on the homes he was building then. He had tried to talk Joe into a new house, had said little when Joe explained he couldn't afford it. Joe couldn't bring himself to tell Babson that the commission the Adams Agency got on the Ali Baba account alone was more than Joe's salary for two years.

He shook his head, wondering if he should phone the hospital, then decided to shave. Staring at himself in the mirror, he scarcely recognized the stranger with sunken eyes and greying hair. Ten years!

It was hard to believe that, at 23, he had been editor of the campus newspaper, with the world at his feet. He remembered the night he had stood on the moonlit grounds, handsome, self-assured, wondering if he should get serious about journalism, or maybe personnel management.

That was when he first saw Ann, a girl in a white frothy dress, with black bangs fringing a white forehead. She had smiled at him; and he had walked with her over to the dance hall. He had kept on walking with her ever since.

"Joe, we'll make the whole world envious!" He could still hear her voice the night he proposed. "Oh, Joe darling, I'll never fail you, not for as long as the stars shine . . ."

"And the rivers run to the sea," he'd ended, with mock gravity. "My little armful, I believe you are quoting Clause 27 of the Blackfoot Indian Treaty."

"Joe!" She'd flung herself in his arms. "Oh, Joe!"

Ann was made for love and loving; that was all you needed. Ten years and five children later, he knew better. He had been grateful for a steady job with Adams. He had died a little inside with every raise he managed. He had quit the crazy dreams about an agency of his own. You needed money for that . . . enough credit to carry you a few months, anyway.

He was drying his face wearily on the threadbare green towel, the last of the wedding linens, when the phone frightened him again.

It was Elkhorn, his voice gruff and tired. "Joe? Couldn't phone you before. We had to perform a section. Everything's alright. You have a fine boy."

"Ann?"

"Okay. A bit weak, though."

"Thanks, Doctor, thanks." Joe wasn't quite sure what a "section" was, but he was sure that this time it had been hard for Ann, really hard.

He was surprised to find, when he hung up, that he was crying. This one Ann would call Joe; she insisted on that, if it was a boy. He was shaken inside, confused.

A high-pitched wail, running to the house, penetrated the tight knot inside him. Only one kid on the whole street had lungs like that . . . Miles.

He came sobbing blindly to the door. "Daddy, Jerry Wilson hit me with a stick . . . wight on the head. An' that hurts, y'know."

There was nothing wrong with Jerry Wilson, except that he was five years old, but Joe felt himself getting mad, the way he always got mad when those he loved were hurt.

"Why don't you hit him back for a change? You're as strong as he is!"

Miles considered it. "He's bigger'n I am. . . ."

"That doesn't matter. Just hit him back!" Joe said. "Like this. . . ."

Miles' big eyes followed his father's fists in fascination. "Dat would hurt him, Daddy!"

"Then he'll leave you alone! Now get out of here . . . Daddy has to work!"

The wash to sort and put in the machine . . . there were still 22 payments owing on *that*. Groceries to get before Shirley came. . . . There was a frantic yell at the outside door. Faithful little Bridget was sounding the alarm. "Toosers has all her hands up in the air!"

"Hold them up!" Joe yelled. "I'm coming!"

Lord, he thought, stumbling up the basement stairs, *Ann can't stand up to this right away again. Shirley can't stay long, I've got to get help for her!*

To every man there comes a moment when desperation reaches a limit. It came to Joe when he was starting lunch . . . a daring idea, a burst of brilliance, a solution so simple it left him weak.

He turned up the gas under the soup, then made a list of his creditors. It was an impressive list. As an afterthought, he inserted Ali Baba Homes at the head of the list.

Praying his confidence would not desert him, he asked Mrs. Ellersby, next door, if she'd mind keeping an eye on the kids for a couple of hours in the afternoon.

Like a man in a trance, he went out to the colourless old car that—like Ann and himself, he thought—had taken a bit of a beating over the years. He drove away from the streets of the subdivision, filled with their skimpy wartime houses, up to the new industrial end of the city, to where the planing mills and lumber piles of Ali Baba Homes sprawled over acres of land.

Mr. Babson's trim young secretary showed him in. The owner of Ali Baba Homes seemed a little surprised to see him.

"Adams said you wouldn't be over today. Said you had a new son."

The enormity of what he was doing was closing in on Joe like a concrete wall. "Mr. Babson . . . er . . . how's business? I mean with credit restrictions and higher down payments. . . ."

Babson shrugged silently, "Joe, you never want to worry about little things like that. People have to eat. People have to have homes. New policies may block the stream a moment or two, but it keeps right on flowing." He looked Joe up and down. "We're building 500 new places this year, all under NHA. You did a good job promoting our homes last year . . . we sold every one before it was finished.'' He added, ''We're building a few private jobs, too . . . more expensive, though.''

''Like the one you wanted me to have?''

Babson looked at him oddly. Joe took a deep breath.

''Mr. Babson, I've been thinking for ten years of the words I should use today. Now they won't come.''

''Shoot, fellow,'' Babson said quietly.

It wasn't easy at first. Then suddenly the thought of Ann, and the crack Adams had made, did something to him. His jaw tightened; and he knew that, no matter what happened to him now, the longest chapter in his life was over.

When he had done, there was a long silence. Then, slowly, Babson swung around in his swivel chair. His face seemed harder.

''You're starting your own agency? Walking out cold on Adams?''

Fear cut at Joe. Fear, foul and sickening, and tinged with something else. He got to his feet, knowing now there was no going back.

''That's it,'' he said flatly. ''Pick up the phone if you want to and be the first to tell Adams.''

Babson smiled. ''I can't understand why you waited so long.''

''You mean . . .'' The reaction was too much. Joe's hands were shaking.

Babson made a gesture. ''What do I owe Adams? But I like you, and I like the way you know how to work. Mind if I give you some advice?''

Joe nodded mutely. He couldn't believe that anything in life could ever be that easy.

''It won't be all pie,'' Babson said. ''But I believe you'll make it, Joe, for the same reason I made a success of Ali Baba Homes. Want to know that reason?''

He could only nod.

''Alice, my wife, waited a long, long time for her first real home. Somehow that goes into every house I build now.'' Babson was smiling slightly. ''That's why you can sell my homes, Joe. You know what people dream of. You can sell automatic washing machines just as easily. You know how desperately today's wonderful young mothers need them. Adams never knew, never will know.''

Babson pulled a blueprint towards him. ''We'll take your wartime house as down-payment on the new one. If you like, the balance can be an advance against the work you do for us. Take a look at this . . . it's my idea of the kind of house a rising young executive needs.''

Joe shook his head. "Mr. Babson, can I . . . can I wait till Ann can listen, too? A woman can dream an awful lot in ten years."

Babson handed over the blueprint. "Take it with you. Tell her about it. Just remember," he said, as Joe reached the door, "anything worthwhile takes something out of you, Joe, but it gives a lot more back."

As soon as he got out of the car, the children sprinted from the Ellersby lawn to greet him, even Toosers who navigated the concrete steps backward, on hands and knees. Joe felt grand and good inside . . . maybe the way a mother felt, after her months of labour and waiting. Only she couldn't . . . his baby had been ten years inside him, and everyone of those anxious days made the joy more worthwhile.

He picked up Toosers first, kissed her and swung her high in the air.

"Daddy," Bridget, jumping up and down, couldn't wait for her turn. "Daddy, I have a real sneak-ret to tell you."

Joe bent obligingly. Bridget cupped her hand over Joe's ear. The gist of Bridget's *secret* was that every morning she was going to be dry, and she was going to give her penny to the new baby.

Joe hugged her. "I've got a secret for you," he said. "You're gonna get a nickel *and* a penny, and the nickel's all for you."

The brown eyes were out of this world. "Daddy, Daddy. . . ." Anything to have Daddy all to herself for a minute longer. "Daddy, do you 'member when I used to say . . . to say. . . ."

"I remember when you used to say 'bedadoes' for potatoes," Joe assured her. "And 'buntons' for buttons, and. . . ."

"Daddy," Miles had struck a ferocious stance. "Daddy, I did what you said."

"What was that?" Joe asked.

"I beated up on Jerry Wilson!"

"What?" said Joe.

"He said he was gonna hit my wittle baby brother on the head. So I slammed him. Boy, I weally slammed him, like 'wis, an' 'wis." Miles' dramatic re-enactment managed to send him sprawling over the boulevard.

Mark stared at him in disgust. Almost indifferently he pulled a brown envelope from under his sweater.

"Here, Dad."

Joe took it. Mark's report card. There was the familiar score of H's . . . Honours . . . the teacher's remarks: "Mark is a very gifted student." Joe held it, feeling suddenly as if it was the most important piece of copy that had ever been put in his hands. *What are grey hairs to a joy like this?*

"If you like," Mark said, scuffing the sidewalk, "you can take it to Mom."

Joe turned up his oldest child's face and saw tears. He put his arm around the skinny shoulders. "I'll sure take it to Mom," Joe said. "Mark, I'm so proud of you . . ."

"Yeah!" Miles had picked himself up enthusiastically. "Marky's weally smart. Marky, if anybody fights you at school, tell me. Boy, I'll slam him, I'll weally slam him!"

"Shettup!" Mark said.

"Boys, boys!" Joe grabbed them both. "I've got a lot to tell you, too, and Mother. You think if Mrs. Ellersby came in after supper, I could slip down and visit Mom?"

"Sure, Dad." Mark squared his shoulders. "We won't let Toosers be scared."

"We sure won't!" Miles made a fearful face. "If any ol' witches come to eat her up, she can just call Miles-y."

"Daddy!" Bridget was yelling from the foot of their steps. "Baby's got all her arms up!"

Joe ran to grab her, thinking of their little son. Another incredible character, no doubt, for an already incredible family.

Ann, Joe thought, as he ran, *today more than one man was born into the world!*

Enchanted Summer

There comes a time when you begin looking backwards—especially, I think, if you were from the northern bush country. Well, I was—and when they started that dam on the Paddle, I went back in memory. As with "The Washing Machine" this story is virtually a slice of life, life as you see it before you grow old.

Susie didn't know it when she chose a homestead site on one of the finest sun-bathing slopes on the whole of the Paddle Hills, but she'd assured herself of trouble. Her doorstep was right on my route to the deep pike pools of the river.

The first day I saw her, I was resting with a couple of straw-coloured jacks, snared smartly from a gold-bottomed shady pool in the Paddle. Snared because the July day was too warm for them to bite—and if there was a law against snaring pike in that distant era, no one ever told me.

I was resting on the hill because it was too nice a day not to sit on a summer hillside. I could hear the skreek of a grasshopper singing against the grasses. And I was aware of something else: the lightest-ever rustle of dry soil at the end of the hollow log on which I was sitting.

My head turned slowly. My eyes met a pair of equally curious eyes, peering brightly from the base of the tree. This was no woodchuck, inspecting an intruder at ground level. This was a skunk—forever to be remembered as Susie.

There were lots of skunks in the country then. Every farmer's dog sooner or later rushed one—to his sorrow—particularly in the fall, when the young take off to dig dens of their own.

Susie was something else again. Big, as I soon discerned, with old age creeping up on her, so she hadn't the speed or litheness for foraging anymore. Her great size was ample warning to grouse and other birds to do their dust-bathing on less-inhabited hillsides. Her family responsibilities must have astonished even herself. The average skunk has from four to seven young. Susie had ten—each one a dainty-footed, obedient, quick-tail-raising miniature of mother.

I don't know what Susie thought as we gazed at each other respectfully that first morning. I know what I thought. Winter. Snow. Fur. With luck, three or four dollars for a prime skunk pelt. A lot of money in the depression era—to a farmer, let alone his son.

"Hi," I said.

Skunks are not unduly concerned about any enemies, even men. But maybe Susie had been raised not to get chummy with strangers. The bright eyes slowly sank back down into the hole.

Careful not to startle anybody, I placed a fish, tail first, at the opening to Susie's summer home. For a minute or two I thought she had been brought up not to accept gifts from strange men. Then suddenly the fish disappeared soundlessly into the earth.

"You get to be a nice fat girl, Susie," I encouraged—the bigger the pelt, the better the price.

Susie was definitely a fish lover, the fresher the better.

In no time at all she started meeting me on my return from the balm-lined river. She was the biggest skunk I have ever seen in my life; I think she must have weighed upwards of 20 pounds, tapering from her narrow front shoulders to a great girth across the rear. Curiously, she had a completely black head: the white stripes didn't start before the nape of the neck. She was so interested in my catch, she'd bump into my legs—the way a cat does when you're carrying a dish of gourmet dinner.

It wasn't long till the young were meeting me with her—all ten of them—parading in single file, all with tails up (proudly, not menacingly). Within three weeks, the whole tribe was meeting me on my way to the river. I had to watch the kits. I had a feeling they were waiting to try out their spray guns.

Skunks have a basic diet of roots and berries. But, like cats, they love meat, normally small rodents. My adopted family—or, rather, Susie's—began to look to me to supply a few of the staples. I asked my mother to save me any rotten eggs and other tidbits she didn't want.

"That's the first time," my mother said. "I ever heard of fish eating potatoes."

"This is for the skunks."

"Skunks!" said my mother. "Is that what I've been smelling?"

"They don't spray themselves," I said. "So they don't spray me. The young ones probably think I'm one of the family."

"There are days I wouldn't doubt it," said my mother. "Be sure to bring back the lard pails."

Susie really liked the porridge.

In retrospect, that summer seems suspended in time. I close my eyes and see it still . . . the dark balms on the river, stirring sometimes in the aimless summer winds . . . the waxed splendour of wild rosehips colouring on the hillsides . . . the young ducks skip-flying around river bends . . . and, incongruously, a farm boy without even a straw hat to shade his eyes, filling his face with saskatoons on the sun-smeared hills, a family of skunks, spread out like spokes of a wheel, digging for roots and rodents around him. Sometimes Susie would pussyfoot towards me, to stop about three feet from my face.

"I think she gets worried that I've died," I explained to my family.

"She's not alone," said my father, who was forever after me to stop daydreaming and get on with the chores.

My parents, born in Ireland, had taken a fatalistic view of my attitude towards farming. Walking after horses, when you harrowed the spring seeding, was irksome beyond words. Racing from school down to the river valley, to see if today there was a white weasel with a black-tipped tail in your trap, was a different thing. They were grateful for the dollars the pelts brought—but I know now they felt the price was high. My mother used to talk to the first old crow to come back to the farm in springtime. (I came by my idiosyncracies honestly.) And my father would throw out wheat for the grouse that came up from the muskeg in winter, to pick around the barnyard in the freezing dusk.

I caught my first weasel at eleven, under an old culvert half a mile from our house; skinned it rather badly—but still got a dollar for the pelt. In that depression, that awed my family. I shot squirrels with a .22, trapped muskrats, snared coyotes . . . and the only time both parents put their foot down was when I started wondering how I might expand into the socially-objectionable world of trapping skunks.

What changed their attitude was the revelation that our new high school teacher—a man my parents held in almost superstitious respect—trapped, too—skunks included. They had only one last objection: how would I keep the smell from getting all over my clothes?

The secret, said the teacher, was to shoot the animals so that the scent apparatus was instantly paralysed. For extra security, you skinned outside and downwind. It worked. The animals were easy to spot—their black stripes stood out plainly against the shrinking snowbanks on the hillsides in spring. I had found out they dug their great grass-lined winter quarters on the very curve of the river hills.

August was coming to a close. There was less joy now in going to the river. I would look at Susie and wonder if, with spring, she would even turn away when I came back to that hillside, my .22 in my hands.

The tall grasses strained and broke in the September winds. The skunks began to prowl about the dry hollows, ravines and abandoned beaver embankments of Paddle valley. The family was breaking up, the young ones leaving to dig their own dens for winter. There they would semi-hibernate, coming out in mild weather, sleeping the sub-zero weeks away.

I found them on every hillside—foraging, homestead-hunting. They knew me—so much so that they scarcely looked up at my coming. They would stand, small heads facing me (rather than looking at me over their shoulders, mortars ready for action).

Once, on a drizzling mid-September evening, a dog left some duckhunter on the river to yodel up my trail to Susie's hillside. I was in time to witness the calm way in which Susie stamped with her forefeet and—when the dog attacked madly, as the dumb ones always do—let him have a virtual jet-spray at the supreme psychological moment. The dog, yelping pitifully, tumbled back down the path to the river. Even I kept to the windward of that route for the next three weeks.

Webs of waterfowl trailed south over the river. By day, the woods were incredibly noisy. By night leaf-scent rose from every hollow.

Somewhere during the harvest time I lost Susie! It was a supreme shock to come up the hillside and see no skunk . . . not even a near-grown one. With my heart curiously speeding up, I looked under the old dead tree for sight of the fine grass gathered so painstakingly to line the winter den. There were only old leaves choking up the entrance.

"Duck hunters," I thought. Maybe the guy with the dog.

"He shouldn't kill them," I said to my father. "At least not unless he wanted the fur!"

"Och now, John," said my father, "nobody would be after killing that many skunks. There's no doubt in my mind that they're out looking for new homes. Skunks, I suspect, are a great deal like people."

At the oddest time that fall, a strange feeling of loneliness would come over me. In the hot haze of mid-afternoon, turning the back-setting with the old gang plow, I would see—crazily—eleven black-and-white plumes on those berry-scented hills. Coming from the barn after doing the evening chores, I'd stare, suddenly, at the thinning bush and the ember skyline—and think of them.

The last wedges of ducks flew low over the barns. High winds stripped the softwoods. And on one such night a fearsome commotion in the hen house brought us running. The coal-oil lantern showed us the culprit—one enormous skunk, even wider across the beam than I remembered her, a whole-black head looking at us from under the roosts.

Susie!

My brother came running with the .22 and I sighted it as best I could in the lantern light. As if the movement called forth memories, Susie turned to face me, one dainty paw held up.

"Maybe," I said, the gun suddenly heavy in my hands, "maybe skunks are like dogs? Maybe she followed my smell."

"John," my father said, "if you don't get rid of that skunk now, she'll never leave the place alone."

There was truth in that—but as I said to my father her pelt wasn't prime yet.

On my orders, my brother tied up the barking dogs. I took two hen eggs, stuffed them generously with red pepper, then got a large cardboard box which I stuck in front of Susie.

"Get in there!" I said.

"John, if that beast sprays you, you're not stepping into the house again," my mother threatened.

But Susie went in—almost gratefully, as if into a refuge.

Ever so gently I pulled the box outside. I stuck the two eggs inside. My fingers touched a warm face. I stood for five minutes, then suddenly the box gave a violent movement. I opened the lid—and Susie took off into the darkness.

When I turned to the house, into the first big snowflakes swirling down against the light of the coal-oil lamp on the kitchen table near the west window, I felt strangely empty. As if I had lost something I would never find again.

What I lost was the magic of a certain summer, when all nature is a boy's kingdom, and everything in it falls under his spell.

I never saw Susie again. The drifts got so deep that winter that nobody could plow through them to the river hills, to look for skunks coming out against the dry grass slopes in springtime. Not that it mattered.

◆◆◆◆

The Trouble
with Eve

This had to be included for what one editor once referred to as my "nutsy humour." The bush country is conspicuous by its absence—but I can tell you some of the grandsons of the pioneers became very much like the principals in this tale of romance in a stock promoters' office. How could it have been otherwise!

Fred could have quoted Scripture to prove the day of temptation would come even to two young and upright investment counsellors like Adams and Anderson—us. I don't think, though, he could have foreseen it coming in the person of Eve Myers.

Our trouble is, we can advise other people on the how and where of investing their money—but we opened up our little venture during the recession. That we survived was due to the people who'd learned to trust us when we worked for the big firms. On top of which, Fred is a born promoter.

"Remember the old Biblical adage," Fred will encourage eager-eyed hopefuls. "Make your shekels increase and multiply, or be held to account for hiding your light under a bushel. But," Fred will warn sternly, "remember the famous Adams and Anderson adage as well— that prudence is a virtue. Stick to gilt-edged securities. Buy value. Be content with a modest profit."

So when it comes to advising *us,* what does Fred choose? Fred always has us try our luck on highly-speculative stuff—the kind of stuff that prompted the VSE to get out the big stick.

Even with a glut of prime office space, our landlord was getting a bit snarky the morning I took the elevator up to our floor, exhausted from two hours of convincing our printers that we'd be settling with them any day for the job they'd done on Blue Mountain Oils—which we were floating exclusively.

I liked the track record of the guys behind Blue Mountain—but what do you do with half-a-million shares when everybody's talking about the price of world oil collapsing because the Sheik of Timbuktu wants more American dollars and so is going to keep the pumps working overtime? The way it looked to me, we unloaded fast or we were finished. Real simple.

That's when I heard Fred's voice coming from our office—and Fred was really warming to his subject.

"Miss Myers, the only way I can explain our forecasts is by quoting that good text: 'And I say to you one man is born with the gift of healing, another with the gift of prophecy, one with a faith that moves mountains and another with powers of stock-market discernment—' "

When I walk in, this lady—sitting properly in a chair, wearing a let-me-tell-you-expensive pin-striped suit (skirt and white blouse ruffled at the throat)—is hanging onto Fred's every word. Blonde, smooth as tickertape—to me she's enough to take your eyes off the quote machine that costs us about 400 a month in rent.

Then Fred coughed—which is when I got that funny feeling in the pit of my stomach. There comes a time when a simple factor may change legit guys into shady operators—and I had the horrible feeling that for us the time had come.

"Meet Miss Myers, Mitch," Fred said. "Miss Eve Myers. Miss Myers," said Fred deprecatingly, "has heard our enviable claim— that never yet have we advised a client wrongly. Miss Myers," beamed Fred, "has some available capital that she wishes to invest."

Miss Myers held out a friendly little hand. "How do you do Mr. Anderson?"

"You can call him Mitch," beamed Fred. "We don't dwell overly much on formality."

"Neither do I," said Miss Myers. "You can call me Eve."

"How much were you thinking of investing?" I asked. "A thousand?"

"Fifty thousand," says Fred blandly.

I threw my briefcase on the counter, the better to avoid Miss Myers'—Eve's—excited young eyes.

We had got in the first offering of Blue Mountain at two-bits, less commission and discount. Currently, B.M. was floundering around the 40-mark. If I read Fred right—and I knew I had—it meant he was figuring we might as well make a few thousand as anyone else. Trouble was, unless B.M. hit the pool that's supposed to feed the tar sands,

Eve was liable to come out of it with about five thousand net—and I don't mean net profit.

"I'll tell you about it, too, Mitch," confided Miss Myers, sort of shyly. "You see, Arthur—that's my fiance—is—er—"

"Mr. Savage—that's—er—Arthur," Fred filled in, "is the cautious type. Mr. Savage," said Fred, raising his voice a little, "is afraid we're far from being out of the recession."

"He says," said Miss Myers, "the collapse of those Alberta banks is proving Fidel right."

"Fidel?" I said.

"Castro," said Miss Myers.

"Mr. Savage read an item—apparently in the *Globe & Mail*," said Fred, "quoting the Bearded One as saying the banks are going down the tube and therefore he wants to put his money in an old sock under the mattress."

"Well, not really!" Eve was blushing again. "He just doesn't want us to lose our security when it's been handed to us on a golden platter."

"Miss—Eve—came into an inheritance," explained Fred.

"The lawyer said it's not all that great for these times, but there were lots of months when I didn't have enough left over from my librarian's salary to afford a T-bone steak. And Arthur says if we make maximum use of this opportunity—pay cash for our home—well, then we can go ahead and get married and the whole economy can fall around our ears, for all we'll need to care."

"You see, Mitch?" said Fred gravely, like a doctor looking at a bad appendix.

I saw all right. Exactly how Fred saw Eve Myers' 50 big ones.

"Grandpa left me the money," Eve said, biting her lip. "The last thing he said to me was, 'It's guys like your Arthur make me partial to the feminist movement. If this doesn't convince him to marry you, I'll roll over in my grave.' " She added, unnecessarily: "Grandpa didn't really like Arthur."

I was developing a sneaky liking for her grandfather. Maybe a little for her, too. Fred coughed.

"That," Fred said, "is why Eve has come to Adams and Anderson. Mr. Savage to the contrary, we believe—with Sir Wilfred Laurier—that this century belongs to Canada."

Miss Myers' eyes—not quite blue, not quite green—were suddenly grave.

"Arthur would have a fit if he knew I was risking our money on the stock market. That's why I thought I should come to a couple of small guys like you. I mean," said Eve hastily, "in addition to your wonderful reputation. I thought some intimate advice from a small firm . . .''

''We understand,'' said Fred gravely. He looked at me again. It was a very significant look.

''Miss Myers—er—Eve,'' said Fred, tapping his fingertips, ''wants us to recommend stocks that are really secure''—there was a slight edge to Fred's voice—''and yet, at the same time, have a chance of quickly doubling in value. That way, she plans to surprise Mr. Savage within a matter of a few weeks.''

From the look in Fred's eyes, I could just imagine how surprised Mr. Savage was going to be.

''There's just one thing,'' said Miss Myers faintly, as if she had suddenly read my mind. ''I keep thinking of how mad Arthur will be if—if Laurier was wrong.''

''Miss Myers!'' Fred looked shocked. ''We endorse Sir Wilfred all the way.''

''Oh, I do, too!'' said Miss Myers loyally. ''I mean, I'm always telling the kids at Keeway Central—that's where I work—to read about great men like Sir Wilfred Laurier. . . . Anyway,'' said Miss Myers, ''it's just that, with Arthur, you can't afford to take chances. So here's what I'd like to do.''

She swung her eyes to us.

''You gentlemen,'' said Eve, blinking her blue-green eyes, ''will recommend a stock to me. If it goes up in a couple of weeks, then I'll ask you to recommend another. Then if that one goes up—well, how could even Arthur doubt any longer?''

Miss Myers made quite a point of apologizing for her seeming lack of faith in our judgement—apparently Arthur had warned her to be doubly careful of investment counsellors.

''He calls them pot-boiler operators,'' said Miss Myers.

''Boiler-room promoters,'' said Fred absently. He caught himself.

''Eve, we *appreciate* such sound business acumen. Firms like Adams and Anderson are not to be confused with so-called boiler-room operations. *We* unequivocally advocate a policy of caution in investment always. However . . .''

Fred closed his eyes, like an undertaker with bad news.

''You are asking us to recommend a stock that will double in two weeks?'' He opened his eyes and fixed them on Miss Myers. She nodded bravely. ''Miss Myers, there is one exchange in Canada where I have seen a stock do that. Unfortunately, it might be off the boards a week later.''

''I—I can't wait forever,'' said Eve. ''I mean—day after day I hand out books to other people's kids—what am I saying?''

"That's all right," Fred assured her. "Perfectly understandable. . . . Eve, will you wait here while my partner and I go into formal consultation?"

He thrust an armful of annual reports at her and pointed to the consulting room. He closed the door.

"Fred—"

"Leave the ethics till later," said Fred, "and pick me something that will skyrocket in a week."

"Over the counter or—"

"Never mind where! Just pick me one."

"Okay," I said. "The only one that I can think of that has a hope is X-R Tech—"

"You know who's promoting that?" Fred almost screamed. "That guy would promote a company to take babies away from their mothers and sell them back for ransom. Besides, high-tech stocks are zilch right now."

"Maybe not this one. You know what they're saying this morning? This X-R Tech has come up with something where you use lasers for filling teeth—no more drilling! It's supposed to revolutionize the dentist business—"

Fred was already out of the door.

"Miss Myers," said Fred, "if you'll pardon the return to formality now that we're down to business, in the mood you're in now, and bearing in mind our words of caution, I'd suggest one stock only—XRT, Vancouver. It's a company that has done some unique research in X-rays for dental purposes—and if the dental community can be convinced that laser drilling beats ordinary drilling on teeth . . ."

When she left, he slumped back in the chair, exhausted.

"Don't say it, Mitch." He lifted a hand at me. "It was another Eve got us into this mess . . . in the Garden of Eden. If it hadn't been for her and her appetite for apples, there'd be no dry holes, there'd be gold in every gold mine, you'd never need bits to grind away at your defenceless teeth—"

That's Fred. But this time I let him talk.

"All right!" He looked at me, finally. "So it's a spec. One of these days they will be using lasers for teeth. Maybe this is it? If X-R Tech goes, and the second one we recommend goes, Eve Myers is going to put maybe the whole fifty grand into our hands. We sell her Blue Mountain. If we don't pick two winners, she won't be back. If we *do*, all I can say is Blue Mountain ought to blow wild."

"Blue Mountain is oil," I said. "Ottawa gives us a great new deal on oil when oil's a glut in the market. Big deal. They'd have to find oil in such quantity that it would justify a new pipeline—"

Fred swung around in his swivel chair.

"Mitch," he said, "I've been thinking about us lately. Nobody has to paint me a picture of the ancient prospector chasing will-o'-the-wisps for twenty years. Mitch—we're them! Only we're decked out in city clothes. Instead of a burro, we have a car. Instead of a shack, we have this front. Instead of heat and flies and sand and loneliness, we have drips like J. Arthur Savage."

Fred's eyes blazed.

"Look at that dame. You know, she's cute. She's got lots of the smarts, too, even if they're a bit old-fashioned. I mean, she knows what she wants—kids . . . an identity in Lonesome Valley or wherever that library is—"

"Keeway," I said. "Poor end of town."

"That figures," said Fred. "That and the grandfather. So, if we're gonna start getting involved in their personal lives, we'll be out in Keeway County, too—picking up garbage. Besides, we'd be doing Eve Myers a favour if we sent her back to that creep without a penny."

Fred got so wrought up, he pounded his fist on the desk.

"Think of it, Mitch! If that first woman had done what she was told, there wouldn't be creeps like Arthur Savage—"

"Fred," I said, "if you don't cut out this archaic ranting, they're gonna haul you up before the Human Rights Commission."

"For what?" yelled Fred. "If you can't call a creep a creep, then I say give Canada back to the Americans!"

The phone cut him short. Fred gets awfully excited when he starts in about Eve—the first Eve, I mean.

The next morning, though, Fred and I got a bit of a shock. XRT-V showed on the machine up forty cents. Before I could get from my desk to his, it had shot up another dime.

"Oh, my sainted mother!" Fred was holding his head. "Those dentists must've gone for it—Oh!"

The screen had started changing figures as if some kid was playing with it.

"Oh, yie!" said Fred. "Why didn't we take that, instead of that stupid Blue Mountain. . . ."

By noon the next day, XRT was well over a dollar. It slumped back to 95—"See?" Fred yelled. "These wild promotions!"—then it really took off. By the end of the week it was over seven bucks.

It was the sort of thing that could finish you if you thought about it. Fred and I didn't. In fact, when Eve Myers came in—so radiant I thought J. Arthur had finally set a date—Fred and I were poring over papers as if handing out advice like that was 24-hours-a-day stuff.

"How can you do it?" Eve said to Fred. "How can you be right all the time?''

''Well,'' Fred said humbly, ''it isn't easy.''

Naturally we had our second recommendation ready and waiting. This time we'd picked a pipeline—one so cash-rich it was a turkey just waiting to be hustled to the thanksgiving table.

''I hear rumours,'' said Fred. ''Notice the way that stock's edging up in volume? Notice who's buying up big gobs of it? And guess who they act for?''

Naturally he didn't talk this way to Eve. Not that it would have mattered. She kept looking at him as if she wanted to kiss him. Fred finally tugged at his tie and broke off in the midst of explaining that it might take a little longer for this one to show results. ''But remember our basic motto,'' said Fred. ''A lot of prudence—a little daring!''

''Oh, I like that!'' Eve said rapturously. She smiled suddenly. ''Mr. Adams—''

''I thought it was Fred,'' said Fred.

''Well—Fred. Do you mind me asking a personal question? Are you and Mitch married?''

''Us? Married!'' Fred gave a cryptic laugh. ''In this game!'' He remembered himself just in time. ''No, Eve, we are not married. If we had stayed within the normal brokerage community, we probably would be, keeping normal hours, going wearily home, complaining about cutting lawns, fulfilling our destiny of earning our bread by the sweat of our brow. Unfortunately, in an operation where we are so close to our clients, so involved in caring wisely for their money, it wouldn't be fair to a wife.''

Miss Myers gave Fred a positively dazzling smile. She lifted her hands as if she had an impulse to straighten his tie.

''Mr. Adams—I mean, Fred—before we get to today's stock selection, I wonder if I could ask your personal advice? I mean, anyone who can choose stocks the way you do—''

Fred recovered. ''Arthur?''

Eve nodded. ''Would you tell me—honestly, please—if you think I'm attractive enough to really interest a man? Maybe I am just an old maid librarian—''

Fred's fingers started to shake again.

''Miss Myers—if I may be formal again for the moment—I'll put it to you this way. If you were a new stock we were promoting, and I described you as 'attractive enough to interest a man,' the Securities Commissions in every province in Canada would nail us for misrepresentation by understatement.''

Eve tried hard to keep on looking uncertain.

''Well, do you think it's that a librarian is just sort of dull—''

"Dull!" Fred was shocked. "Custodian of the greatest thoughts of the greatest minds—dull!"

"Well, then, why is Arthur so—well—hesitant?"

Fred backed off a foot and looked her over. To show her it was a strictly professional analysis, he frowned intently and scrutinized her from one angle, then from another. Eve Myers looked more worried by the minute.

"Well?" Her anxiety was genuine.

"Well," said Fred, "I'll tell you frankly, I think Arthur's resistance is a twentieth-century phenomenon. He's one of those persons who doesn't know a sound stock when he sees one."

At least, that got us back to investments again.

Fred dangled his long legs from his desk and talked about pipelines in general and Pacific West in particular. Eve Myers perched herself on the adjoining desk, crossed her legs, and looked radiant.

"It's wonderful! Your whole life, I mean! It's like gambling—only safer."

Fred took a deep breath. "You approve of gambling, Miss Myers?"

"Arthur—I mean Mr. Savage—doesn't," I said.

Fred and Eve Myers looked around at me, as if they'd forgotten I was there. Miss Myers got off her desk and tugged slightly at her skirt.

"Yes. As Arthur says, when a person substitutes hunches for intelligent reasoning, it's time he was locked up."

Fred kicked a wastebasket across the room after she left.

"I'd like to lock him up! I'll bet he doesn't take her out on a picnic without a written guarantee from the weather bureau."

"And where," I asked, "is all this getting us?"

Fred stuck his chin in his hands glumly.

"Mitch, let's be realistic for a change. What chance have we of even seeing her again? Pacific West's a beaut of a stock, but even if the takeover talk is true, it could be months. . . ."

The philosophical look came into his eye.

"See, if that first Eve had behaved herself, we'd *know* when the takeover would be. Like a cow knows when there's gonna be an earthquake."

There are times when Fred's store of unrelated knowledge hypnotizes even me.

"And this Eve," Fred went on, "wouldn't even be interested in a drip like J. Arthur Savage. She'd see a nice guy, fall in love with him, marry him. It would be impossible for her to fall in love with someone who insisted they couldn't get married till they'd saved up enough money to pay for a house." Fred fingered his chin. "Furnished, he says now!"

"I don't believe it," I said.

Fred looked at me severely. "Mitch, you know what your trouble is? You oughta read worthwhile books. All you do is pore over those stock reports and stuff. Start reading your Bible!"

I did. I read all through Exodus when Pacific West took off. It was about 18 the day Eve came in. In exactly ten days of high trading, it hit 28 (the directors doubled the dividend, trying to stave off the takeover). Not bad for a blue chip, as I said to Fred. Better than a slap in the belly with a cold fish, Fred said. We might even have rejoiced a little—if we'd owned any of it . . . and if what we did own hadn't been dropping a penny with each passing day—Blue Mountain.

"The thing I can't figure," said Fred, on the twenty-second morning after Eve first came, "is why hasn't she come back? You'd think she'd be choking us with fifty thousand-dollar bills, screaming at us to invest it so Arthur would get off his you-know-what and lead her to the altar." He gave a savage snarl. "To think I beat my brains out to make money to let that jerk get a wife the sandals of whose shoes he is not worthy to tie!"

Nobody can misquote the Good Book with effect like Fred can, especially when he gets wrought up.

Eve came in that afternoon. She had a new outfit, right down to a hat. A hat can make a man—or even two men—stare these days.

It was Fred who got his eyes off the hat first. He bounded to her. "Eve! You've been crying!"

Eve closed her eyes and nodded. "Yes. That's why I bought the hat. You need a new hat when you're gonna cry all day."

That kind of logic failed even Fred. Suddenly he gave a jump that almost landed him on the ceiling.

"Arthur found out!"

"Yes," Eve sniffed.

Fred calmed down. He circled Eve once—warily.

"How'd you get away from the library at this time of day?"

"I worked till eleven o'clock last night, and I finally got the French cards done. So they let me take the afternoon off."

"And you told Arthur you wanted to invest in our next recommendation?"

Eve started to cry a little. "Fred, will you ever forgive me?"

"For what?" Fred yelled. "What on earth would I have to forgive you for?"

"I feel like a wanton woman—"

"Well, everybody gets feeling that way." Fred relaxed a little. "Even Mitch and me." He amended it a little. "Everybody, I guess, except Arthur.''

"But you don't understand," said Eve. "Arthur kept telling me you couldn't trust anybody—that everybody would be trying to get my fifty thousand dollars. Do you see?''

Fred didn't, but he nodded. There wasn't much else he could do.

"Well," Eve said, "I told myself: 'If I test you on two stocks, you'll be sure to recommend two sure-fire ones.'''

"How," said Fred, "did you ever believe anybody could recommend two such stocks? If it were that easy, every broker would be a millionaire. Did you ever meet a millionaire promoter or broker?''

"You're the only people I've ever met who work at giving investment information. Unless you count insurance people and—''

"I understand," said Fred. "What happened?''

"So," said Eve forlornly, "I put twenty thousand in that laser company—I didn't want to take too big a gamble—''

Fred nodded. I thought he might faint as well.

"And I wasn't greedy," Eve said. "As soon as it doubled, I said: 'Sell!'''

"Very prudent," Fred managed.

"Then because Pacific West is such a good stock, I put everything—well, almost—in there. Then I got cold feet. I thought it would double, but my broker said it would be wise to sell at least a portion, so I sold it all at fifty per cent profit.''

Said Fred: "We always encourage independent thinking. So if you don't mind my impatience, what the hell's eating Arthur?''

Eve's chin trembled slightly. "I couldn't stand deceiving him. So last night I told him we had enough to buy almost any house we wanted—furnished. And he—he—''

"He what?'' Fred was almost screaming again.

"He says: 'Listen, kid, you got the Midas touch. Another haul like that, kid, and we can both quit our crumby jobs.' We had an awful fight. I gave him back his ring. . . .''

"You know," Fred said, a little wonderingly, "you did what every Eve has done since the beginning of time. You took a gamble, thinking you'd make the man you love happy—and you lost.''

"Please!'' Eve said. "Don't sympathize with me. Or I'll cry.''

"Let me give you one last piece of advice," Fred said. "Don't buy any more stocks. Buy Sentinels—or Canada Savings Bonds—well, maybe some blue chips. . . .''

Eve nodded, sniffing.

"I was going to invite you—and Mitch, too—around for my first dinner in that new house. But that's out now. I just have this awful feeling that if I kept on investing, Arthur would want to keep on till we could buy West Edmonton Mall. He's gone crazy over the stock market!''

It took awhile to get Fred out of the shock of it.

"It's better, Fred,'' I said. "We couldn't have looked at each other if we'd sold her Blue Mountain."

Fred finally looked at me.

"Mitch, grow up. Neither of us was ever going to sell her Blue Mountain. It was just another will-o'-the-wisp for two desert rats to follow."

He clenched his fist. "It's that rat Arthur I'm mad at—'

As if on cue, the door opened and a fellow with a black derby and umbrella walked in. He rapped authoritatively on the counter.

"Mr. Adams or Mr. Anderson, please."

I cut in ahead of Fred.

"My name,'' the fellow said briskly, "is J. Arthur Savage. You have been highly recommended to me by a friend."

"Thank you, Mr. Savage,'' I said, loudly enough to drown Fred's strangling noise.

"I have come for your current recommendation,'' said J. Arthur Savage. "Something sound, of course, yet with outstanding speculative prospects."

"Would you come into our consulting room, Mr. Savage?'' I said.

When he was seated, I leaned over, waxing confidential.

"Mr. Savage, have you ever heard of the legendary oil pool that, some geologists feel, feeds the McMurray tar sands? A pool so enormous that alongside it the pools of the Middle East are dwarfed into insignificance . . .''

That was a bit over two months ago.

Since then, Fred is more his old self again. He's spending a lot of evenings with Eve, looking over some rare books she has. At least that's what he says he's looking over.

And as you may have heard, Blue Mountain has brought in an oilfield of such magnitude that the petroleum pundits can't even agree on its potential.

What really hurts is that J. Arthur Savage has all our shares.

You Gotta
Go Home Again

This, too, is taken from a composite of many things observed and heard over the years—not the least being the memory of an interview (for a business magazine) with a very successful man who left the bush country and who, for for half-an-hour each Friday morning, was never interrupted till he had finished reading the old weekly newspaper from "back home."

Almost 46 years from the drizzly Saturday in September when he left Avalon to work as a raw roughneck for Tri-West Petroleum, Joe Devlin returned. The unreal years were behind him. Fittingly, rain was falling over the bush country.

Mile after rain-soaked mile of big black hay coils and sodden wheat swaths rolled by. Pity, born of long-forgotten fear, sprouted inside him again.

"Why do they stay?" he asked himself.

For that matter, why was he coming back?

No Devlins around Avalon any more. Mike was in Ortona, Mary married an Australian, Pat retired to Campbell River. Their parents, Wild Bill and Wanda, had died without ever seeing Indiana again.

When he was a kid hunting muleys down draws like these, he'd noticed a funny thing. An old muley, when he sensed that death was near, would turn back home to die. A lot of Joe's pals from the oil patch had been dying lately.

But, being honest, there was that bit in the Avalon *Echo* about Howie Parman, too. Shannon had nobody now, either. He wanted to touch base with her and with his own boyhood. Lay old ghosts to rest.

"Why not?" he said, thinking of Shannon. "Our lives are over, anyway." What harm in seeing her again?

He stopped for a minute on the crest of the hill. Avalon lay below him, shrunken and blurred under the sullen rain. A farm pickup passed him, the tires licking up wet from the asphalt. The young driver stared unseeingly ahead, his face as bleak as the rain.

"I know, kid," Joe said, and eased down to the valley.

He didn't need to ask if there was room at the hotel. He rang the small bell long and hard before a girl emerged from the cafe area. His name meant nothing to her.

"Who's got the poolroom now?" he asked.

"Baldy Pickering," she said, and went back to the cafe.

Baldy Pickering had been in the second grade when Joe went away. He hadn't really changed—just grown fatter and balder. He was unwrapping rolled-up girlie magazines, rolling them the opposite way, then spreading them along the wooden display shelves under the TV. Before Baldy there had been a radio up there.

"How come you didn't come out to open the library?" Baldy said. "The way the *Echo* played up your donation—"

"Something came up," Joe said. He didn't want to explain to Baldy that when he went away, it seemed the most important thing in the world that he show Avalon the Devlins weren't predestined to be hard-luck farmers forever. By the time he could donate the library, somehow that wasn't important anymore.

"Out for anything special?" Baldy was eyeing him. Maybe he remembered that Shannon had been the only girl Joe ever dated, before she took up with Howie.

"Got a big shareholders' meeting coming up," Joe said. "Wanted to unwind a little."

"Uh-huh," Baldy said.

"And maybe touch base with the past," Joe admitted. "They say everyone has to make a trip back home sometime."

"They didn't all do as good as you," Baldy said. "Remember Keewee Watson?"

Joe remembered. Keewee had talked of being a big-league baseball pitcher some day. He always played in the First of July Sports Day, always sure a scout from Toronto, maybe even the States, would spot him.

"Know what he's doing now?" Baldy put more magazines up on the rack. "Next time you drive to your suite of fancy offices in the Esso Tower, drive along 105th Avenue—you know, by the railway tracks? Good chance you'll see Keewee, pushing a grocery cart full of empties down to the bottle depot."

It had been a long time since anything had hit Joe Devlin as hard.

"Remember old Altmann?"

The auctioneer. The only person Joe remembered as having money in those depression years. When he walked around, even when he was auctioneering, he jingled it in his pants pocket.

"Ever hear how he got his start?"

Joe couldn't recall that he had.

"Freighting cream for the farmers down south. His first customer was his own mother. He charged her, too."

Altmann had suffered a stroke, had died without a friend.

Major Martin was gone. Joe remembered him in a blue serge jacket, his World War I medals pinned across the front, leading a pathetic little group of veterans to the Legion Hut on Armistice Day. . . . Miss Wilson, their grade-school teacher, had never married—too old when the depression ended and another war came. . . . Most of the farm kids he had known had retired, some to the Senior Citizens Lodge in Avalon, some to Edmonton, most to British Columbia.

"Jamie Lindstrom," Joe said. "I think he married Ellie Parsons—"

"Hah," Baldy said. "You know they had a kid kinda late in life— sort of an afterthought, if you know what I mean. Well, the kid's got leukemia. They don't figure she's got a year left to live."

In the second-floor room of the hotel, he stood for a long time by the window, scarcely seeing the scattered lights of farm buildings smeared with the wet blackness of the night. From his wallet, he fished the *Echo's* brief account of Howie Parman's passing.

> . . . lifetime residents of the Avalon community, Howard and Shannon were not blessed with children of their own, but gave enormously of their time to all our young people's activities. Howard Parman was a fine citizen and good neighbour to all who knew him.

"And that's it?" Joe said. "A good neighbour to all who knew him? So goodbye."

He took a sleeping tablet before crawling under the cold covers. He was no longer sure it was a good idea to come home.

He didn't go all the way to the farm the next morning. The rain had stopped, the skies stayed sullen and low. The blind-line road was still impassable. He pulled to the side where it made a T with the gravelled range-line road. Half a mile to the south was the old Morrison place. They had better land than the Devlins; but if anything, the Morrisons were poorer. There were no boys to help with the land or to trap down in the bottoms or to work out for a dollar a day. It was here

Shannon waited for him to join her on the way to school—even if it was winter and 40-below. . . . Crazy kid!

One memory in particular came back to haunt him. He was in high school, fed up with her trailing after him.

"Wait up for me, Joe!" she'd called to him.

He turned and saw her—really for the first time. A skinny kid in a flour-sack dress, half-running and holding her side.

"You walk so fast, my side hurts."

Sometimes he tried to beat her to the corner, but he never walked that fast when she was with him again.

Sitting in the car, the rain tapping dismally on the roof again, he had a desperate yearning to turn back time. To say to his father: "For one year, you don't have to fix anything with haywire!" To tell his mother: "Don't worry if the frosts come early! This fall you're not going to get up at midnight and go out and cover the tomatoes with old sheets and papers." Only the greenhorns from Indiana would take land the wiser ones knew as jackpine soil, where the wheat never went more than twenty bushels an acre and the first frosts got you every autumn.

Six mouths to feed! No wonder Wild Bill had ranted about the politicians on both sides of the border. And how had Wanda ever picked enough berries to last them the winter?

"Dear God!" Joe said. "How did you do it?"

He turned his car, to head north of town, up past the sandhills to the old Dutton homestead. Howie Parman had made a down payment on it when he took Shannon there as his bride. That was two years after Joe left Avalon. The only thing that surprised him was that she had waited that long.

Howie had fought a losing battle with the years, Joe could see. The fence posts sagged, the barbed wire was slack. Howie had never managed an electric fence. There was enough of Wild Bill Devlin in Joe to make him feel a nameless anger.

Shannon was in the kitchen, wiping a water bucket full of freshly-gathered eggs. She stood up and stared at him almost uncomprehendingly—no bigger, he would have sworn, than when she used to wait for him at the blind-line corner. The wet rag dropped on the kitchen table and suddenly she was bawling against his shoulder.

"It was the debt and another wet fall." They were having tea at the kitchen table, and she was telling him about Howie. "It costs so much just for a tractor now—"

"Even for an oilman's bombardier."

"Howie went out and saw the grain sprouting in the swath—and he came back up to the house—'' It was hard for her to continue. ''He said, 'I feel kind of funny, Mom. . . .' You know we didn't have any children, but we used to pretend that if we called each other 'Dad' and 'Mom'—''

''Don't, Shannon,'' he said gently. ''Don't.''

''It helps to talk.'' She dabbed at her eyes. ''Just like that, his heart gave out.''

She wanted to know about him. Joe told her as best he could. Of the years as roughneck . . . a swamper's helper . . . of teaming up with another Irishman to form a contract drilling company . . . of saving their money and starting their own oil company.

''We got listed on Calgary,'' he said. ''We had a lot of savvy—but we were babes in the wood. We went under—and I mean under.''

The years of saving again—but with a difference. They knew where the oil *should* be now. This time when they went public, they were listed on the Toronto exchange.

''Seven of our first eleven wells came in. We never looked back.''

''So,'' Shannon said slowly, ''you really don't have to worry anymore—''

''Well, it's never that simple,'' Joe said. ''Right now I've got a gut feeling about a takeover bid. That's why this annual meeting is so important—''

''Joe,'' Shannon said, ''if you had it to do over again, would you do it the same way?''

''If I had it to do over again,'' he told her honestly, ''I'd ask you to marry me—even without a cent—especially without! We'd have made our couple of million together. And if we hadn't—''

''It wouldn't have mattered,'' Shannon said.

''No, it wouldn't,'' Joe agreed, a little wonderingly. ''We'd have laughed at life—like my mom used to laugh—even in those skid-shack towns where the roughnecks fenced in a piece of ground around the trailer the way the homesteaders used to fence in the first gardens.''

She said, later:

''I don't have to tell you there never was anybody but you. But I wanted someone to care for—kids to love—'' She was near tears again. ''Howie was a wonderful man, Joe—''

''The Howies of the world are the heroes of the world,'' Joe said. ''That's what they should have put in the *Echo*.''

''The only thing that really scares me is not having anyone to care for anymore. I wouldn't have minded if Howie had been an invalid all the rest of his days—'' Suddenly her face was crimson. ''Joe, it doesn't even seem decent to talk like this. But you have come home—''

''Yes, Shannon,'' Joe Devlin said heavily. ''And maybe I shouldn't have. I'll put it to you straight. I made a mistake when I left you back then—I had seen your mother and my mother go without all their married lives, and I just couldn't do it to you—"

She was looking at him in bewilderment.

"What are you trying to say, Joe?"

"I thought I had nothing to offer you then," Joe Devlin said. "Now I know I have nothing. I'm an old man, Shannon. Men five years younger than I are dropping dead—"

"Oh, Joe!" She put her hands over her face. After a long moment, she spoke again. Her voice was quiet. "Maybe you're right. For a minute there we got caught up in the silly romance highschool kids know. Thank you for coming, Joe. It was kind of you to call."

"Ah, hell!" he said, driving back to Avalon. "To hell with the whole rotten mixed-up mess people can make of their lives."

"We're sure proud you come for supper, Joe." Jamie Lindstrom was as big and red-faced as his father had been. "You're Avalon's only real success story, you know!"

"I'm the Devlin kid from the scrub farm four miles west of here. Remember? I just happened to make a few bucks along the way."

" 'Tisn't that simple" Jamie said. "You make anything out of your life, you gotta put out."

They were in the Lindstrom's living room. The TV was on. Ellie and Kathy were in the kitchen, doing up the dishes. The girl reminded Joe for all of the world of her mother back in grade four. A bit paler—and with a dignity that could break a grown man's heart.

"Jamie, remember the year I was twelve?"

"Something special I should remember?"

"A weasel trap," Joe said, and Jamie's mouth dropped open. "Your dad had taught you how to trap, and I was so fed up with us never having a cent for anything. . . ."

The year came back to him with all its pain and shame and the utter frustration of poverty. He'd tramped miles against the paring February wind, trying to sell Gold Medal seeds for ten cents a packet—three cents for him if some sympathetic farm woman had a dime left to buy. In the fall, their whole crop froze; his father couldn't even get him the few schoolbooks he needed. It was in November that he went to the hardware store and asked the proprietor to sell him a 20-cent weasel trap—on time.

"Nothing on time," the storekeeper said flatly. "Especially to—" He'd been going to say "a Devlin," Joe was sure. He looked away. "To kids."

He told Jamie again of the scheme he had thought of on the way home from school. There were weasels everywhere; the cats kept dragging up the remains from the slough below the barn. Joe figured if he took a mousetrap and baited the wooden release with chicken blood, a weasel would put his head down to taste the blood and the spring would be strong enough to break its neck.

He pestered his mother to kill a chicken, fastened the trap as he had envisioned it a thousand times.

He raced home the next afternoon from school. The trap was gone. The snowshoe rabbits were cycling, and one of them had taken it along with him, securely fastened to one big hind foot.

Jamie Lindstrom laughed at the memory. "I wonder how long he did hop around with it?"

"Then I set the trap you lent me under that culvert half-way down the blind-line road—"

"Where the rabbits wouldn't get into it?"

"Yeah!" Joe agreed. "And I was lucky." Lucky in trapping, he thought now, as later he was lucky in oil. He caught a weasel the first night, skinned it badly, and the storekeeper gave him a dollar-fifty for it. Joe Devlin vowed then he'd never be poor again.

"They were tough years," Jamie Lindstrom agreed. "With a capital T."

"I owe you," Joe said.

"Grow up, man! You owe me nothing."

"I owe you," Joe repeated stubbornly. "Only I never knew how to pay till now. Maybe I could do something for Kathy—take her to the Mayo Clinic—"

"Joe," Jamie said, "with medicare and everything, they've done all they can for Kathy. They're holding the leukemia pretty well in check. You just have to accept that you can't make life the way you think it should be. Life just can't be pre-planned!"

He was a man giving voice to truths he'd learned only from life itself. "I don't understand the why of these things—though sometimes I think I get a glimpse. If we only had good times, who could stand us after awhile? We'd be puffed up, proud—nobody could stand us. Nobody would ever need us—then what would we do in this world?"

He pulled at his nose.

"With Kathy, we don't know for sure how long we're gonna have her. So even little things—like doing the dishes together—have meaning. For Kath, it's the same. . . ."

He was having difficulty speaking.

"You know what she wants for her birthday? A pup . . . And I'm so slow to learn, I keep thinking: 'What do we do with a dog when she's gone?' I think that baby of ours can read our mind. Because you know what she said to me, Joe? 'Daddy, nobody knows how long he'll live. I'm going to live longer than lots of people driving home tonight.' That's pretty profound for a kid.''

''That's pretty profound for anybody,'' Joe Devlin said.

It was late when he got back to the hotel. He phoned, anyway. Shannon's voice was low.

''I'm leaving for the city in the morning,'' he said. ''I have things to do—like fight a takeover bid, for instance.''

''That's why you phoned?''

''No. Among other things, I want to look up a guy we used to know. Remember Keewee Watson?''

''Joe, Keewee hasn't been sober for years!''

''Maybe if somebody just talked to him—got him to dry out— sometimes you never know. What I'm trying to tell you,'' Joe said, ''is that if you owe life, you gotta try to pay the debt.''

There was silence. Easy, not strained.

''Joe, am I reading too much into what you're saying?''

''You couldn't possibly. I'm coming back—unless you say no.''

''Joe, maybe it has been too long—''

''Oh, it's been too long,'' he granted. ''But I learned today that's the wrong way to look at life. Shannon, you and I, right now, have as much as any two people in this whole world. You know, good memories can make the present that much more meaningful. And we have all the rest of our lives before us.''

A long time later, he went to the window. The bush country seemed changed—strangely beautiful. The rain had stopped. A full harvest moon was shining.

''Frost!'' Joe said, stabbed by those long-forgotten fears again.

But when he pulled up the window, the wind was warm—a caress from the western hills.

''Two, three days of that,'' Joe Devlin said, ''and the combines will be hurrying around those rows again!''

He had built an oil company on hunches. And he had a hunch now there'd even be a spell of Indian summer—the right time to be coming back again.